REQUESTED TRILOGY

PART TWO

# until

# you're

# mine

by Sabre Rose

For more information about the author visit:
**www.sabreroseauthor.com**

ISBN: 9781791894931

**Taken. Broken. Captive.**

There used to be a small amount of safety

within the walls of my cell.

Not anymore.

Now my body is broken and bruised.

And he doesn't come to comfort me.

I ache for him.

His face dominates my dreams.

His body dominates my desire.

Then he offers himself to me and I lose myself in him.

But I do not love him.

I cannot love him.

To do so would risk my chance at escape . . .

*This story contains dark scenes of a sexual nature.*
*Reader discretion is advised.*

"The thing about music is when it hits you feel no pain."

- Bob Marley

# CHAPTER ONE

## REQUESTOR

I bang on the doors, causing them to rattle in their hinges. I try the handles again, pulling down and yanking hard, but they won't budge.

"Father!" I roar.

If I calmed down, if I silenced myself, I would be able to hear his muttered words through the doors, but I am beyond that point now. The need to know what has happened consumes me, the pressure inside my chest enveloping my being until I want to burst from my skin and rip the doors off their hinges like a fucking monster.

"Fath—" I'm cut short by the doors finally opening and my father appearing in their place.

"Keep it down, Junior. You'll worry your mother."

The anger inside seethes at his words and I take a measured step toward him. "What happened to her?" The words are hissed through my clenched jaw.

Father takes a step back, just one, but with it I see his hesitation. I see it flick across his eyes. In this moment, my father is scared of me.

And he should be. I tower above him in height. I spend hours in the gym developing my strength. He is nothing compared to me. He is old and wrinkled and weak.

Well, he would be wrinkled if he hadn't injected his face with too much poison. Even as he looks at me now with fear licking his irises, his expression is impassive, vacant. Just like the rest of him. Regaining his composure, he pushes past me.

"She's fine," is all he says.

Fine? She's fine? I just heard him talking to Ryker, the man who has my songbird, and he used the word 'wounds'. 'Wounds' is not fine. 'Wounds' implies pain, damage, brokenness.

My jaw aches with how hard I'm clenching it as I follow him through the maze that is our house. "What happened to her? If Ryker has hurt her or done any—"

"Ryker has done nothing but his job," my father snaps.

I picture Ryker in my mind, his smirked-filled face, his stupid tattoos and scruffy beard, and then I think of my hands wrapped around his neck, squeezing and squeezing until his face reddens and he's clawing at my fingers, desperation filling his eyes as he realizes that this is it. He will die by my hand. Literally.

My father's voice snaps me out of my fantasy. "I won't be telling you anything until you calm down."

I stop walking and take in a deep breath, counting to ten. Apparently, it's supposed to help. It doesn't. My blood still pulses in my veins. My chest thuds with the trapped beat of my heart. My skin tingles.

"I'm calm," I tell him. I'm not, but to all outward appearances, I am. I've trained myself to be this way. Trained myself to hide the truth of the monster that simmers within.

"It wasn't Ryker." My father stops in the hallway, leaning against the wall as he speaks to me. His voice is lowered, hushed. "It was Marcel."

The humming sound of blood increases and I have to step closer to hear his next words.

"He broke into her cell last night."

My songbird needs me. My sweet, sweet songbird has been touched by another man. Abused. And he will pay. Just the thought of it alone spikes my blood to boiling point again but I use all my strength to stop if from boiling over and dominating my actions.

"I need to see her." I keep my voice low and controlled, matching my father's.

He shakes his head. "It's not a good idea at the moment. Give her a few weeks to heal."

My anger leaps and I struggle to maintain control. "I want to see her!" I bellow, my rage barely contained. I ball my hands into fists, relishing the feel of my nails sinking into flesh.

"You know what you're like, Junior. There is no way—"

The pain in the palms of my hands gives me something else to think about. Something to lessen the buzzing in my ears. "Do not tell me what I am like, Father. You cannot keep her from me. She is mine."

"She will be yours," my father corrects. "I will not have you putting our family at risk by having her here too early. Look at you now. Look at the way your body is trembling with anger. You're barely holding it together. What if she were here? What if she were the one to piss you off?" He steps closer; any of the fear I saw in his eyes before has vanished. "What would you do to her?"

We glare at each other in the dark hallway, each waiting for the other to back down, step away. His gray eyes bore into my blue. But I am the one to relent. Until my father is gone, he is the one with the control. He is the one the staff listen to, the one who has the police in the palm of his hand, the one with friends in the right places.

Taking a step back, I cross my arms over my chest. "I want him dead."

My father turns away, walking down the passageway. "Who?" He talks as though he's already forgotten.

"Marcel." My jaw aches.

"Because he hurt your girl? He's not used to—"

"Not because he hurt her, because he touched her. She is mine. I agreed to your stupid stipulation that Ryker give her some basic training, but that brute, Marcel, was never supposed to be near her. He wasn't supposed to know she existed. He must die."

My father laughs. He laughs. And it infuriates me. This

wouldn't be happening if it were one of the whores from his collection. If someone had touched his beloved Lily without his permission, they would be dead without hesitation. Ryker would be called and the person, whoever they were, would be let go. Let go into the dirt.

"We are not a big operation, Junior. Marcel is valuable to us. When we bring the girls to auction there is a certain level of submission required, and Marcel excels at—"

"I don't fucking care what he excels at or how valuable he is to your little operation. I want him dead." My voice is an explosion, debris hitting the walls and igniting my veins, but my father merely narrows his eyes.

"Now if you'd only calm—"

"What if it were Lily?" I control my breathing, attempting to steady myself in the face of such disrespect.

My father sighs, admitting the small defeat. "I will call Ryker and discuss it."

We're in the kitchen now. My mother sits at a small table in the bay window, sipping on wine as the cooks scurry around her. Her lips are already stained and it's only early afternoon.

I glare at the back of my father's head, having visions of grabbing the cast-iron fry pan dangling from the rack above the bench and bashing it against his skull until he is nothing but a mess of blood and pulp on the floor.

My mother looks over at my father dispassionately. "What are you calling Ryker about, hmmm?" She does that. Adds a little hmmm onto most of her questions. It's meant to disarm, meant to create suspicion and my father falls for it every time. Idiot.

He shifts uncomfortably, his eyes flicking to mine in some sort of warning. I don't know why, though. My mother knows everything that goes on in this house. There is nothing hidden from her.

"Nothing you need to worry your pretty little head about, my love." My father places a kiss on her cold cheek.

She rolls her eyes and looks over to me for an answer.

"Marcel touched something that's mine."

My mother blinks once and slides a strand of ice-blonde hair behind her ear. "Then he must die." She shrugs, and I almost want to hug her. Almost, because I don't like to be touched. It makes me feel trapped.

She doesn't care about the staff scuttling around us, and from their lack of reaction, I guess there is no need to.

My father clears his throat, an attempt at a power-grab settling in his expression. "I will be the one who deci—"

My mother lifts a single brow to silence my father, and he walks out of the room, already pulling the phone from his pocket to call Ryker. I wish I had her power, the ability to bend him to my will with the simple movement of a brow.

Turning to me, my mother smiles and pats my cheek. "All better?" she asks.

I sit at the table next to her, slumping my head into my arms. Her hand rests on the back of my head and strokes my hair in an attempt to soothe me. It doesn't. My anger is subsiding but not quickly enough. I keep envisaging Marcel with his hands around the neck of my songbird, his mouth on her lips, his—

I sit back up abruptly as my pulse starts to race again. My mother's fingers are still tangled in my hair.

"Play for me, hmmm?"

"I don't feel like it," I snap back, blinking rapidly, trying to get the vision of my songbird with another man's hands on her flesh out of my mind.

"But it will make you feel better." Her fingernails are sharp on my scalp and I push into them, wishing her to claw harder. I don't like to be trapped by touch, but this is okay.

"You can play anything you like." She smiles sweetly. It's a strange look on her. Not one I see that often. There's a part of me that wants it to be genuine, but I know better.

"Fine," I say like a petulant child.

Scooping her glass off the table, she glides out of the room, the translucent folds of her gown flowing behind her as a mist of silver. I follow meekly, through the warren of hallways until we get to the music room. Across the hall, the doors to my father's office are closed again, though I can't hear any voices now.

"What do you want to hear?" I take a seat at the grand piano, pushing my feet down on the pedals, testing their resistance.

"Play your emotions." She leans against the lid of the

piano, taking a sip from her glass of wine. "Play what's inside you right now."

I let my fingers settle over the ivory keys and listen to the song within my soul. It is dark and filled with rage.

My fingers start to move, finding their own way across the keys as if under no direction. I jump from bass to treble. Back and forth, slowly, adagio, gaining momentum until pausing before the main development, the climax. Then my fingers fly across the keys, increasing in tempo and passion, forte to fortissimo, until my entire body sways, my fingers hitting the keys with force. I finish triumphantly, already the music of 'O Fortuna' having worked its magic of transferring the torture of my soul to the ivory and the strings.

My mother looks at me impassively, one hand gently clapping the palm of her other. "Well," she takes another sip of her wine as though the music hasn't moved her at all, "you're nothing if not dramatic, my dear."

She turns on her heel, ready to walk away, but I call out to her, suddenly scared of being left alone with my thoughts.

"Would you like to hear another?"

Already, dismissal is etched on her face, but before she can leave, I press my fingers to the keys again, playing one of her favorites. My mother may not have a talented bone in her body, but she can appreciate good music when it suits her, and there is nothing she likes more than musical theater. Ever since I was young, she's dragged me along to every performance in the city. I never want to go. I hate the people around me, the way their bodies press to mine due to the closeness of the seats, the way they sit unmoved, but eventually that fades away as the music enraptures me.

Like 'O Fortuna', the theme song of 'Phantom of the Opera' doesn't have the same gravitas as if performed on the pipe organ but I do what I can, watching as my mother's eyes roll back in her head, her chest rising with the intensity of the music.

I mimic her, closing my eyes and picturing the day my songbird will be here, singing for me, my very own angel of music.

mia

# CHAPTER TWO

## MIA

There used to be a small amount of safety within the four walls of my cell. But not anymore.

I still know everything it contains. I know every rough patch on the floor and the exact location of the red pebble. I can find it by feel. I tested myself once, on my hands and knees, fingers searching the floor until I was confident that the red pebble lay beneath.

I know the arc of the sun and the moon and how the square of light will spill across the room, over the floor, and the shape of its distortion when it touches the walls.

I know the stars that travel across the sky, not their names but their patterns, the ones that blink on and off. But I no longer think God is watching. It would be too cruel if He were.

I know the level of shampoo left in the bottle. I know how far to twist the faucet to stop it from dripping. I know the shape of the watermarks that stain the walls.

But now it seems foreign. It no longer feels safe. I watch

the red light of the camera, knowing that if it flicks off my nightmare might begin again.

There is nothing to tell what is beyond that door, whether it leads to more doors, just like mine, or if Star and I are the only ones here. Or if she is here at all.

I haven't strayed from the bed since Ryker left. I'm lying in patches of blood that have seeped into the sheets from each time I shift. My entire body pulses with pain. I cannot escape it. I can feel every lash of Marcel's belt across my skin, and each time I swallow, the pain is a reminder of his fingers around my throat.

I long for relief, for Ryker to come back and hold me in his arms, or at least to give me a painkiller. My prayers are answered when the beeps of the keypad sound and the door sighs open. But the face that rounds the corner isn't that of Ryker's. Instantly, I recoil from the stranger, but when Ryker walks in behind him, my racing heart calms.

"Ah, yes." The man walks over and kneels beside my bed, placing a case down on the floor and opening it to peruse its contents. "What was used, may I ask?"

He talks to Ryker and not me. In fact, the man doesn't look me in the eye at all. His gaze floats over my body then back at the case lying on the floor. Ryker hasn't looked at me either. It's like his eyes are glued to the man at my side, as though there's some magnet that keeps his gaze away from me.

"Leather belt," Ryker says. His eyes flick my way, just

once, and so quickly that had I not been staring at him, I wouldn't have noticed at all. "Studded," he adds. He swallows and his Adam's apple bobs up and down in his throat.

The man kneeling on the floor draws in a whistle of air and shakes his head. He's rifling through the contents of his case. His glasses keep slipping down his nose. I lean further over on the bed, wincing at the pain it brings, but manage to see what's in his case. He must be a doctor of some sort. I allow myself a small smile when I see the collection of pills and potions in his case, desperately hoping that he will give me something to relieve the pain.

"Is she allergic to anything?" Again, the doctor looks to Ryker for the answer.

Ryker shakes his head, this time his eyes caught on the ground. "Not according to her file."

The doctor nods and tips a couple of pills from a pottle into his hand. "She'll need water," he says to Ryker.

As Ryker leaves, I beg him to look at me. I need to see into his eyes. I need to know what he is thinking, why he won't look at me. But he doesn't even give me a backward glance.

The doctor instructs me to lie on my stomach as he examines my wounds. He makes tutting noises and shakes his head, but he doesn't speak to me. When Ryker walks back in, the doctor takes the glass of water from him and tells me to take the pills. Even with the water, they are painful as they slide down my throat, but I don't begrudge the pain as I know it will bring relief.

Ryker leans against the wall behind me, out of my line of sight as the doctor continues. He draws blood. He takes swabs. He listens to my heart and my lungs and records the pressure of my blood.

"When was her last cycle?"

Ryker clears his throat. "She's been here for ten days. Nothing in that time." His voice is low and gruff.

The doctor merely nods and presses a needle into a bottle, drawing the liquid into the syringe.

When he goes to inject it into my arm, I jerk away. "What is it?"

The doctor doesn't answer and instead wraps his fingers around my upper arm, holding tightly and pulling me back toward him. I tense, resisting his grasp and the doctor turns to Ryker.

"Hold her still, would you?"

It is only then that Ryker actually looks at me. His eyes lift slowly, and I'm once more struck by the torment they hold. Dark clouds are gathering in their depths, but I don't know what they mean. He swallows once and turns his gaze to the doctor.

"What is it?" he asks.

Letting go of my arm, the doctor passes him a note. "My list of instructions," he says. "Now will you hold her?"

Ryker scans the note then nods and walks around to the

head of my bed, lowering his hands to hold me in place. I try to move away but the pain stops me.

Tears prick my eyes. "I just want to know what it is."

Ryker shakes his head, but when his fingers wrap around my arm to pull it toward the doctor, his touch his gentle. Almost apologetic. The needle pierces my skin and the liquid is pushed into my flesh. I feel nothing but a cool sensation in my arm.

Placing everything back into his case, the doctor gets to his feet, his eyes falling over me as though I'm nothing more than a body on a table.

"She will be fine. It will take a while for everything to heal but as long as you regularly apply the cream, I don't anticipate any scarring or permanent damage. I will leave you with more painkillers and some cream and some bandages to attend to her. But I would suggest you use a less aggressive method for submission in the future."

I expect Ryker to protest at the doctor's words and insist that it wasn't him who inflicted this, but Ryker merely nods and follows the doctor toward the door.

"Ryker?" I say, my voice barely a whisper.

He stops for a moment, but his back is to me and he doesn't turn.

"Ryker, please look at me."

My words get caught in the base of my throat, as though Marcel's fingers are still there and trying to stop them from escaping. There's a slump to Ryker's shoulders that I haven't seen before, but he still doesn't turn.

And I've never felt so alone as when he walks out that door. I want to beg for him to come back. If I could handle the pain, I would kneel before the camera in perfect submission and hope he saw. Anything just to make him come back. Anything to feel the safety of him. Because if he is here, Marcel can't hurt me.

No one can.

Except for him.

He gets stuck in my mind and I can't escape him. I wonder who he must be outside these walls, if he has people that care about him, a person who is waiting for him to come home. I wonder about his childhood and what sort of life he must have had that has made him forget. From the hesitation in the way he treats me, I know he is battling something within. Something that torments him.

When the painkiller begins to work and I find a few moments of sleep, it's Ryker's face that haunts my dreams. But in them we aren't trapped in a cell. We are free. We are together. And we are happy. And when I wake, I'm not sure which hurts more. The pulsing thud of pain dulled slightly by the pills, or the realization that my dream will never be true.

But when the hushed hiss of air enters the room with the opening of the door hours later, it isn't Ryker who appears. It's Star. My heart starts pounding, scared that Marcel will follow, but the door eases shut behind her and I let out a sob of relief.

She doesn't look at me as she walks over to the bed, tray in hand, her eyes trained obediently to the ground even though it is just the two of us. She's dressed in a night slip like I am. Like I was, before Marcel tore it from my body.

I'm trembling under the blanket. Ever since his attack, I can't seem to get warm. The room is kept cool at all times, but my body had become accustomed to it, regulating itself to adjust. Now, it is as though the cold has seeped into my bones, although my skin is on fire.

Star kneels beside the bed, lowering the tray to the ground. "I've brought you some food." Her voice is soft and gentle, barely a whisper. "And some cream for your wounds." She still doesn't look at me. I want her to. I need her to.

"Star." It feels like years since I've spoken. My voice is broken and torn. The bruises around my throat make it hurt. "Star," I say again, begging her to look at me. I need someone to remind me that I'm still here.

The bruises on her sides have faded to yellowish-brown. Remnants of black circle her eye. The left side of her upper lip is still slightly swollen, but the cut is healed, clean from blood.

She plays with the food on the tray, rearranging it so none of the fruit touches. "Are you hungry?" she asks. And then she lifts eyes so pale it's as if they have no color at all, and they lock on mine. There is nothing behind them. No emotion. No desperation or fear. Nothing but acceptance.

A sob lodges itself at the back of my throat. I cannot

become like her. She's given up. Accepted her fate.

"You should eat." Gingerly, she picks up a slice of apple and holds it out to me. It hovers in front of my mouth, waiting for me to open. All the fruit has already been sliced. Ryker usually brings a knife. My dreams have often been stuck on it.

I'm lying on the bed, resting on my side, unable or unwilling to move. I don't open my mouth but stare into her eyes, searching for the girl who must be in there.

"Eat whenever they offer food. You don't know when it's next coming."

Except, I did. Ryker appeared with food three times a day. But from the way Star's skin was stretched over her bones, I knew it wasn't the same for her.

Slowly I open my mouth and she pops in the slice of apple. My jaw aches when I chew, and the sweetness starts gurgles of nausea in my gut.

"Eat," she says. It's not a command. It's a request. A plea.

I chew and swallow, tears smarting as the apple slides down my throat.

"You've got to keep up your strength," she says. "There's no place for stubbornness here. It will get you nowhere."

I swallow the last of the apple and open my mouth again when she offers another slice. I'm not sure why she's feeding me, but there's something comforting about it. Reminds me of Mum.

"How long have you been here?" I whisper.

She looks at the camera. The red light is on. But for some reason, she answers. She leans forward, so close that her breath hits me as she speaks.

"I don't know. It's a while." Her voice lowers even more, something I didn't think possible and I have to strain to hear her. "No one wants me," she says.

There is sadness there, as though she wants to be sold.

"You haven't been requested?" I ask.

She shakes her head, holding out another slice of apple. There is a hint of jealousy to the set of her jaw.

"How many girls do they have here?"

She shrugs. "It's hard to tell."

I become desperate for information, firing questions at her as quickly as they form in my head.

"Do you know where we are? Do you know who runs this place, any of the names other than Marcel? How did you get here?"

But she ignores my questions, picking up another piece of apple and playing with it between her fingers, seemingly becoming transfixed with the redness of its flesh.

I sigh, knowing my questions will go unanswered. "You can eat it if you like."

Without hesitation, she pops it into her mouth, and it's the first time I've seen any emotion from her. Pure bliss.

"I was larger when I came here," she explains. "Marcel controlled my food in order to help me lose the weight." There's no malice in her voice, in fact, it's almost as though she's grateful. "Maybe next auction I will be sold. Maybe it will be to someone kind."

I swallow my repulsion. "Does he hit you often?"

She shakes her head. "Only when I need it."

"When you need it?" I just about choke.

She nods, picking up another slice of apple and offering it to me. I shake my head and she puts it into her mouth without prompting.

"It took a while for me to learn to behave." She smiles sadly. "Don't be like me. This will happen time and time again unless you learn to obey." The apple seems to have given her energy. She smiles, her movements are less stilted. "Roll onto your stomach. I'll put cream on those wounds."

I do as she requests and brace myself for the feel of her fingers on my broken skin. The cream is cold, but she is gentle. Once she's done, she leans in close.

"What did you do? Why isn't he doing this?"

"What do you mean?"

"Marcel is always the one to look after me when I'm in pain. He's always the one to soothe my wounds. You must have done something really bad if they are making me do it instead."

"It wasn't Ryker who did this to me." I move my head so I'm looking directly at her. "It was Marcel."

Her hand stills on my back. "Marcel?" There is a hint of pain in her voice. "Marcel did this to you?" Her eyes well with tears.

I nod, watching her closely. She's upset.

She swallows, her eyes falling to the ground. "Did he touch you in other ways too?"

With her words the feel of his erection pressing against me, his fingers inside me, come flooding back. A slick cold sweat covers my body and my heart starts to pound, the rush of blood deafening. I draw in a deep breath and let it out slowly. When I open my eyes again, she's staring directly at me, waiting for my reply. And that's when it occurs to me. She loves him.

So I shake my head, wanting to spare this girl any pain I can. "I wouldn't obey. He was punishing me for disobedience."

She smiles. It breaks my heart.

Gathering a towel from the tray, she wipes her hands clean, gathers everything she brought with her and gets to her feet. "The cream will help." Walking toward the door, she pushes it open, then looks back at me. "Next time," she says, "just submit."

"Star?" Her eyes narrow a little when I use her name again. Or, what I assume is her name. She hasn't told me any differently. "Have you seen him?"

She frowns, and her lips pinch together, turning them white. "Marcel?"

I shake my head. "Ryker."

"He's the one who sent me in here to look after you."

I shuffle up on the bed, propping myself up on my

elbows. "So, you've seen him?"

And that's when I hear it. The eagerness in my voice, the desperation to hear about him.

Star's frown flattens. Her head tilts to one side but she doesn't need to say anything. It's all there in her expression.

I'm just like her.

# CHAPTER THREE

## MIA

For days it is only Star who enters my cell. She brings me food, tends to my wounds, and supplies my painkillers, but she doesn't speak like she did that first time.

I miss Ryker. Something broke in him after Marcel's visit. Something that gave me the courage to speak, to ask him why. I thought it had been some sort of breakthrough. I thought he had opened up, telling me about his past, his sister.

But I am nothing to him.

My wounds are healing. I can sit without it causing excruciating pain. But no Ryker means no training and, as pathetic as it sounds, at least it gave me something to do, something to focus on other than myself.

Other than Ryker.

I cannot stop thinking about him. His face dominates my dreams. His body dominates my desire. Trapped in this room, all alone with nothing to distract me, I need to think of something else.

Anything but Ryker.

So I think about the ring of the register each time I keyed in a sale at the bakery. I used to hate that sound. It was the soundtrack to my nightmares back when my nightmares were only dreams. I think of the line of people that sometimes reached the door of the shop. I think about my mother and my father out the back, their hands buried in dough, their faces covered with smiles. I think of Roxy with her lips wrapped around a cream donut, the powdered sugar dusting her cheeks.

I never thought there would be a day when I longed to be working at the bakery. When the sound of the register pinging open would bring comfort instead of boredom. But that was because I was innocent and naïve. It was before my dreams became nightmares.

Five days pass before he walks back into my room. I am desperate for him, desperate for his touch, his attention. My eyes fly open. My heart leaps and without hesitation, I drop to the ground, kneeling in front of him. I don't lower my head though. I sit with my neck craned upward, scanning his expression, needing to see him.

I don't want him to be angry. For the last few days I haven't been able to get the memory of his lips out of my head. They were so soft and gentle, a contrast to everything else in my life.

I want to taste them again.

He looks down, his eyes dark and clouded, and runs a

finger down my cheek, sending shivers of pleasure through me. Such a simple movement, hardly a sexual one, but it does things to me that I never thought possible in this place.

"I haven't given you the command." He takes my hand, lifting me to my feet. "How are you?" he asks. "Did Star look after you well?"

His beard has been trimmed close to his face, his hair cut shorter. I don't want to talk about Star. I don't want to talk about Marcel or my requestor. I want him to take me in his arms and kiss me like he did before. I want him to hold me to his chest, murmur words that rumble through me and make me forget everything about my life but him.

"Where have you been?" I ask.

Taking my hands, he toys with my fingers. "I needed to sort a few things."

"It wasn't because you were angry with me? Because I won't do it again. I won't talk to you like that." I wince as the words come out of my mouth, reminding me of the desperation of Star.

He shakes his head and lets one of my hands go to rub his face wearily. "I needed a few days to clear my head. Figure things out."

"And have you?"

He steps closer so there is only a fraction of space between us, his chest rising and falling heavily. There's a pained expression on his face.

"I can't free you. I can't betray them. It's not that simple.

27

You can't just walk away from this. I thought it wouldn't get to me. I thought I could do this and not think about what it means, about what happens next. I've always been able to sort of block things from my mind and never asks what happens to the girls when they become someone's plaything."

It's as though he's looking for my approval, or at least my understanding, but right here in this moment, none of it matters. It's like my mind has become numb, stuck on him and nothing else. All I can think about is how safe I felt when his arms were around me. The desire that twisted within when his lips pressed to my skin. I know it's wrong. I know I should be pleading for my freedom, my escape. And I fight against the feeling, but it won't dissipate. It's there, like a thundering cascade of emotion that I'm trying to block with a feeble stone in a hole too large.

"I've done many bad things. I'm not a good person. When I look at you, I see everything the world should be and isn't. I see goodness and kindness, innocence and beauty. And I wish I could give you that world, take you back there as though this never happened. But your world is not my world. My world is filled with cruelty and fear, people who own everything and those who must obey them. I've always done what has been asked of me because the risk of disobedience was too high. So, in a way, I'm just like you. But my chains, the walls of my cell are invisible. And your world, this world of innocence and beauty, it's gone.

Forever. You can never go back there."

As I stare at him, I know tears well in my eyes. I hear the words he says, I understand the meaning behind them, but they are blurred by his beauty, his closeness. He reaches out and tucks a strand of hair behind my ear. I want to nuzzle into the warmth, lose myself in him.

"I thought I could do this. But then…" He draws in a shaky breath, his body trembling as though he is the heart-shaped stain on the carpet and some unseen presence is slowly tearing him apart. "But then," he whispers, his voice so raw, so broken, "it was you."

There is a storm of emotion in his eyes as he stands before me, his gaze unflinching. I move a fraction closer and feel the exhale of his breath. My insides are tossing and turning, caught in the undertow then rising to the surface only to get sucked under again.

My memories scream. He chained me. He lashed my skin. He forced me into submission with his actions and yet, here I stand, longing to touch him. Longing to know what it would feel like to forget, just for a moment. Forget who he is. Who I am. Where we are. Forget the horror that faces me, the life I've lost, and drown in him.

Lifting a trembling hand, I run my fingers down the side of his face, through his stubble. Under my touch, his lips are soft, softer than I remember even though it has only been days since I tasted them.

There is a question in his eyes. Uncertainty mixed with

pleading. I tilt my head to the side, my gaze flicking between his eyes and his lips, trying to resist at the same time as knowing it is impossible. I inch closer and kiss him. Softly.

My heart soars when our lips touch and reckless abandon floods my veins. When I cup his cheeks with my hands, he doesn't stop me. His eyes dart over my face, resting on every freckle, every line of my skin, and then I kiss him again. Hungrily. Passionately. As though I've been trapped underwater and he is air itself. His fingers graze my scalp, threading into my hair, cupping the back of my head and pulling me closer. My heart is pounding now, crashing waves of rapture against my chest.

Then he pulls away, hands still threaded in my hair, eyes darting between mine, lips bruised red. His hands drop to his sides. He takes a step back and then he sinks to his knees, lifting those storm-filled eyes, dragging them so slowly up my body it turns what's left of my resolve to a quivering mess.

He's offering himself to me.

Kneeling.

Submissive.

Willing.

Taking his face between my hands, I bend down to kiss him, catching his bottom lip between my teeth roughly and leaving it bruised. I run my hands through his hair, my thumbs over the deep lines of his brow until the temptation of his lips are too much and I lower my mouth, taking his kisses, his desperation and his submission, and losing myself to desire.

As I lower myself to his lap, I tear the shirt from his body, tossing it to the side and running my fingers over his skin. The raised lines of ink swell under my touch. I taste him, running my tongue over his shoulder. Salt and mint and pine. His shoulders are perfectly formed, smooth and sculptured, decorated in ink. I drag my nails down his back, leaving white lines that turn red. He breathes deeply, his chest expanding before he lets out a low moan that reverberates in my core. His skin skitters as I explore, following the dips and curves of his body. Pressing myself closer to him, wrapping my legs tighter around his waist, his hardness surges against me. I push him to the ground, powerful with need. Sitting on top, I press my hands to his chest, grinding myself against his hardness.

The world disappears. There are no walls. No cell. No chains. No prison. There is nothing but Ryker and me and this heated electricity that pulses between us. I fumble with his belt, jerking it off and tossing it aside like I did his shirt. His jeans are next, tugging them down his legs, along with his underwear, leaving him naked and exposed, spread on the floor beneath me as I stand over him.

He is glorious.

Even though his eyes are scorched with lust, he doesn't move, he doesn't reach for me, instead, he watches as my eyes devour him, drinking in every inch of exposed skin. His cock twitches in response when I fix my gaze on it and he groans again, unashamedly letting me know the surge of desire crashing through him.

Pulling my dress over my head, I lower myself to the ground, wrapping my hands around his ankles and moving so slowly up his body it makes him tense and squirm, his hands forming clenched fists at his sides. I run my fingers over the inside of his thighs, applying more pressure when I reach the grooves of his pelvis, touching everywhere and everything but the place he desires most.

My hands keep traveling up his body, over the hardness of his stomach, the rise of his chest, the dips of his shoulders, my body stretched over his but not touching. The torment in his eyes is clear. He's resisting the urge to grab, to take. Resisting the urge to be in control.

I don't need to guide him into me. He's hard and ready, so I hover over him, allowing just the tip of him to brush against me. I'm trembling, quivering in anticipation as I sink further. He's hard and thick and I suck in my lower lip, biting it to stop from crying out. His eyes roll back and he bites his bottom lip too, almost as though he's mimicking me. His hands clench and unclench at his sides as I lower myself onto him an inch at a time, allowing the sensation of him filling me to spread slowly through my body.

Once I'm impaled, relishing the feel of him, I take a deep breath, adjusting to his fullness and his hardness. Even though his body is tight and taunt, held still by sheer willpower alone, he moves within me, growing even harder as his eyes focus on mine.

As I begin to rock back and forth, I lift his hands to rest on my hips. His fingers dig into me painfully. But it's a pain I desire. A pain I want. His muscles flex as he attempts to pull himself from the ground, but I shove him back, an exhaled huff of air escaping him from the force. Holding my hands against his chest, I lift myself, instantly feeling the loss of him, then lower back down slowly.

He's caught between rapture and torture.

Again and again I do this, rising and falling, locking my eyes on his as the threads of his neck strain with the effort of denied control. His fingers twist and pull at my skin, needing something to release the pressure building.

When I dig my nails into his chest, he lets out a hissed whistle of air. Running one hand over the skin of his collarbone, I come to rest on the base of his neck, rubbing the flesh and feeling the bounce of his throat as he swallows. I increase the pressure, gripping my fingers, tightening his allowance of air, craving control. He moans again but doesn't stop me, choosing to keep his hands on the flesh of my hips.

I squeeze tighter, daring him to stop me, daring him to dominate, but all he does is watch me with those possessive eyes, his skin flushing the tighter I squeeze. His cock surges inside me, begging for friction and I rock my hips, watching him curiously as he struggles for breath.

When I finally let go, his hand whips out and grabs my left wrist, twisting it away, causing a sharp pain to knife through my shoulder.

I slap him.

He grunts, jerking his hips upward, pushing further into me. His eyes close and his face pulls into an expression of exquisite agony. Bending myself down to brush my lips over his neck still red from the grip of my fingers, I whisper in his ear.

"Take me."

Instantly, his hand wraps around the back of my head, cupping it as he rolls over, pressing my back to the ground and rising on top as though my command has been what he's been waiting for, the only thing stopping him for devouring me. He plunges back in without hesitation and I whimper as he buries his head between my breasts, inhaling the scent of me.

At no time do I think about where we are. Who he is. What is to become of me. I am lost in the sensation of being filled by him, desired by him, taken by him. He moves me easily, and just as quickly as I was on my back, I find myself lifted to be cradled, my legs wrapped around his waist, our bodies slick with sweat, his cock hard within me.

We writhe together and I thread my hands through his hair, pulling his mouth back to mine in feverish passion. He kisses every part of me he can reach, running his lips over my mouth, cheeks, neck. His hands dig into the flesh of my back, ignoring the wounds which are still healing. But I don't care. There is no pain. Only pleasure.

Gripping the sides of my face, he holds my head still, pressing his forehead against mine and looking deep into my eyes. Our breaths mingle. Our bodies rock in unison. Pressure builds within.

Threading his hands around the back of my head, he tugs my hair, yanking my head backward and exposing my neck. He jerks and thrusts, and an explosion ignites, bursting through the cells of my body as fireworks. He's made me come before, but never like this. Never with him deep inside me. Never with our bodies in a tangled mess of sweat and limbs and passion.

Never as equals.

He stills as he watches the waves of ecstasy roll over me. I move my head back to look at him, an uncontrollable smile creeping over my face. He returns it, his hand pushing the back of my head forward in order to kiss me lazily. He starts to pull out.

"What are you doing?" I ask, pushing back into him, holding him within me, not wanting this connection between us to be over. "What about you?"

"I don't want it to be about me," he says as I start to kiss his neck, gently biting the soft flesh just under his ear.

"But what if I want it to be?" I'm rocking my hips, forcing the friction between us. He's caught in the moment, unable to answer as he fights the urge to come.

"It's too soon. No protection," he grunts or hisses or moans.

I hadn't even thought about it. It seems so inconsequential here, now, but I know he is right. It brings the world back into the focus. The walls of my cell come crashing back into place. The monotone colors blur my vision. But I don't want to be here. I want to be lost in him. A place where I am free to act as I please. A place I can demand his attention. A place I can take control.

He's watching me, lust and desire etched on his face. Before, his emotions were hard to read, just a storm in his eyes, but now it is like the sun has come out, the waves have calmed, and the water is clear.

He's looking at me unabashedly. Unashamedly. Openly.

Untangling myself from him, I pull him to his feet, lowering myself so I can take him in my mouth, wanting to see that loss of control ripple through him. But he stops me, shaking his head and pulling me back to my feet.

"Not on your knees," he says.

For some reason tears spring to my eyes. My heart swells and I launch myself at him. He catches me as I wrap my legs around his hips, kissing him as though my life depends on it. Maybe it does.

"Mia," he groans.

Pulling away, I lift my hands to cup his face. "You've never said my name before."

He grins and kisses me again, before pulling away and

repeating my name. "Mia."

It sounds so beautiful on his lips.

Adjusting himself, he lifts me enough to enter me again.

I smile, running my thumbs over the lines of his brow. "Ryker."

He grunts, thrusting into me, but there's a smirk on his face. "Mia," he says again, but this time it's more of a moan.

It's such a strange thing, but there's something powerful about saying our names, claiming who we are in this prison. Walking us backward, he slumps against the wall. His hands move to cup the cheeks of my backside and he moves me, bouncing me on his cock as our mouths fight for dominance. Then, pulling himself from the wall, he walks over to the bed and tosses me down. I laugh as I bounce and he grabs my ankles, pulling my legs over the side.

"But me kneeling," he says as he lowers himself to the ground, "I'm good with that."

His hands work their way up the insides of my thighs, pulling and massaging the flesh. I prop myself up on my elbows and watch as he lowers his mouth and runs his tongue along my clit. Pulses of pleasure rip through me and he moves closer, pulling me toward him, gripping onto my flesh with desperation as his tongue works magic.

Moving so my back is supported by the wall, I run my fingers through his hair, pulling him closer. He moans and I am undone again, gasping and panting and squirming as the pressure releases.

"Ryker!" His name explodes from my lips as I arch in the air, my body tight as an orgasm tears through me.

He lifts his head and crawls over me, hovering above my spent body. "I dreamed about hearing my name on your lips like that, shouted in a moment of ecstasy."

Lazily, I reach between us and take his steel-hard cock in my hands, stroking up and down and watching as he fights the need to come.

"Fuck, Mia. Be careful."

I stroke harder and faster, intently watching his face and his body's reactions as the sensation begins to overwhelm him. His face twists into exquisite agony. The threads of his neck strain. The lines of his forehead deepen as he bites his lip. He jerks, convulsing as his warm seed spurts onto my stomach. And then he slumps over me.

Spent. Undone.

Our hearts beat in unison, mine just the slightest echo of his.

I breathe deeply, relishing the feeling of completion and satisfaction as I run my fingers over his back. I cross the patch of stars on his shoulder, tracing the diamond shaped pattern. I run them over the dragon that graces his shoulder blade and down to the unmarked skin of his lower back. There is a scar there. Puckered and circular.

"How did you get this?"

He lifts himself and rolls from me, but his head rests in the crook of my arm. He takes my hand and brings it to his mouth as he speaks.

"It's nothing," he says with his lips brushing over my skin. There's something in his tone that warns me to not ask any more. So I don't. I don't because I don't want to leave this moment, this foggy haze of chosen ignorance. Sitting up, Ryker runs his hands through his hair before turning to look back at me. The mess of him is smeared across our stomachs.

# CHAPTER FOUR

## MIA

I wake stretched across Ryker, my head pressed to his chest, my arm trailing across his torso. My leg is bent over his, and the steady beat of his heart echoes in my ear. We are crammed together in the small bed but I wouldn't have it any other way.

For the first time since I got here, I don't wake with dread pulsing through me. I don't have that moment of confusion, thinking I'm home and safe in my own bed before reality crashes.

Ryker sleeps soundly and I nuzzle into his chest, inhaling the scent of him. He smells of cherry blossom today. Just like I do.

Closing my eyes, I think back to the night before and the way Ryker washed himself from me, running the cloth over my body almost reverently and the way he got distracted, his mouth crashing into mine with feverish passion and pushing me against the shower wall to plunge inside me again.

The memory wakens something deep inside, arousing my

desire for him again, so I trace a circle around his nipple, hoping to wake him. His hand rests protectively on my back and his fingers stir a little, pressing into my flesh, but he doesn't wake.

Tilting my head to rest my chin against him, I stare up at him sleeping peacefully. The lines across his brow are faint in sleep, more suggestions of lines than the deep grooves I'm used to. His beard is closely shaved now and not the unkempt mess of before. But his hair is in disarray. His lips are the same deep pink as always, the fullness of them drooping slightly. They look so kissable. Walking my fingers up his chest, I run my thumb over his bottom lip. It turns into a smile as his body tightens and stretches.

"Morning," he says, his hand gripping me tightly and pulling me closer.

"Morning," I whisper back, afraid if I talk too loud I will somehow undo this bubble of bliss. The normality of it, of waking up in bed tangled in Ryker's embrace as though reality does not exist, brings a knot to my throat and I bury my head into his chest, breathing deeply, willing myself back to that place where the walls around me don't exist.

Reaching for me, he tilts my chin back up so I'm looking at him. And then he kisses me, pressing his lips against mine with a rough softness that tingles deep inside. He's lazy with the kiss. Lazy and demanding at the same time. The arm wrapped around me tugs, pulling me on top of him, pressing his hardness into the base of my stomach.

And then he just holds me.

I allow myself to wonder what it would have been like if we had met at a different time. Would he have noticed me? Would I have noticed him? Would we still be tangled in each other's embrace?

He's older than me, at least I think he is. It's hard to tell. There's a hardness to his features, but it fades when he smiles. He might have looked at me and seen just a girl. I might have looked at him and seen just a man with a messy beard and without the storm of conflict in his eyes.

I know my attraction to him is fueled by the intensity of my situation, I try to keep reminding myself of that, but it doesn't change the way I feel right now, here in his arms. It doesn't change the fact that my heart pounds or that desire twists when I think of him. Or the fact that he is my savior and my tormentor all rolled into one.

Or the fact that I want him.

I wonder what he does when he's not with me. What he did before me. But I don't want to ask, because to ask would be to bring that world into our own, and right now I don't want that.

I am content in my naivety. Content in my chosen ignorance. There's a part of me, the trusting part, the doe-eyed part, that wonders how I didn't notice it before. How I didn't see his perfection.

His hands begin to massage the flesh of my back, moving across me like he knows every inch of my body. And I suppose he does. Never before has a man known the contours of my physique like Ryker does. Never before has a man made me feel the way he does. I am inexperienced in the ways of men. Thomas, my only boyfriend, thought that saying, 'hop on' was foreplay.

Threading my arms beneath him, I hook them up and over his shoulders, holding onto him tightly, scared he might suddenly vanish, scared to wake up and find this is all a dream.

Scared that it's not.

His hands move down my back, gripping the flesh of my backside and pulling me further up his body, enough so I have to let go and rise to meet his gaze. He kisses me once. Twice. Then tilts his head, taking my breast in his mouth and caressing the soft flesh with his tongue. Waves of desire twist within and a moan escapes.

His attention turns to my other breast, his tongue coiling around the nipple time and time again until the sensation causes my toes to curl and I press myself into him, almost suffocating him with my flesh.

With his hands gripping my sides, he pushes me up and back so his hardness presses into the base of me. I'm already wet and his eyes roll back in his head as I slide over him. His cock stands proud and tall, glistening with my moisture. He strokes himself once, twice, before moving and guiding himself into me.

The fullness of him is rapture. I take a deep breath as I

sink onto him, bending myself over and clinging onto him as he begins to move. We stay like that, rocking back and forth, our bodies pressed so close together that I don't know where he stops and I start, until the ecstasy is too much and I cry out, sinking my teeth into his shoulder, knowing the flash of pain will cause him to become undone.

"Oh, fuck," he hisses, holding me tight, not moving a muscle as he pulses within.

I can feel the surges of him, the convulsing as he comes. And it's only when he stills again that I move, pressing my lips to his before slumping back on top of him.

We stay like that, with him inside me and my body pressed to him as the patch of sun creeps across the floor. Neither of us talk. Neither of us want to face the reality of what we've done.

It isn't until the patch of sun is midway across the room that he stirs again, withdrawing himself and getting to his feet. He stretches high into the air, his muscles sliding under his skin and causing his tattoos to dance.

"I shouldn't have done that. I shouldn't have put you at risk. The doctor said it would be at least seven days until the injection was effective."

So that's what it was. Contraception. Even though I know I should be worried, I'm not. I don't care. In this moment, I'll take any scrap of happiness I can. To think about the future, about what's to come, simply hurts too much.

Ryker looks over at me cautiously. "I'm sorry. It was

selfish and stupid of me. I should know better. I will call the doctor." He runs a hand through his hair. "I should have never—"

"It's been six days." I don't want to even think about it. "It will be fine."

Ryker sighs. "You want coffee?" he asks, so normally, so ordinarily.

"Coffee? I would die for some coffee." Just the thought of it alone causes saliva to pool in my mouth.

Picking up his jeans from where I had thrown them the night before, he pulls them on, then reaches for his shirt, but I jerk it from him, shaking my head. My eyes drag themselves over his body, wondering how such perfection could exist on a man. He's not handsome, not in the classical sense. He's rugged and splendid and perfectly made as though he's cut from the finest stone. Stone which fell from heaven itself.

I nod and he turns toward the door, eliciting a sharp pang of panic within me at his departure. I want to call out for him to stop. Wait. Don't go. But I say nothing. Because there's nothing I can say. Instead, I reach for the blanket from the bed and throw it into the air, letting it fall to cover the ground.

He returns moments later, a tray laden with fruit in his hands and places it in the chair he used to sit in. Grabbing the coffee cups, he places himself down on the blanket beside me and the aroma wafts into the air, causing my stomach to knot in anticipation.

"Now that I've told you about my sorry excuse of a childhood, tell me about yours," he says, staring over the rim of the cup as he brings it to his lips. His soft, full, kissable lips. But even his lips can't draw me away from the scent of the coffee. I inhale before taking a sip, letting the bitter liquid slide down my throat.

"Oh my god, I had forgotten what sweet, sweet nectar this is."

I take another sip and then another, ignoring the scalding temperature that greets my tongue. He's watching me intently, waiting for the answer to his question. But for some reason, I don't want to talk about my life before. I don't want to drag the memory of my family and friends into this place. I shrug.

"There's not a lot to tell, really. My parents are still together, stupidly in love." I lie back on the blanket and shrug again as though thinking of them doesn't cause me pain. "They own a bakery. There's not a lot else to tell really. I mainly keep to myself."

But he persists. "Surely there must be more to your life than your parents?"

"You probably know everything anyway," I say, thinking of the times he's told me that they know everything about me. If they know it, surely he does too. But I tell him about my love for music, my feeble attempts at singing.

He looks over at me gingerly, toying with his bottom lip

between his teeth and causing sinful thoughts to come to mind.

"Would you sing for me?"

His request catches me by surprise. It seems wrong to sing here. Like music and this place simply can't exist in the same space.

"Here?"

A smile creeps across his face, smoothing out the lines in his forehead. "Yes, here."

Clearing my throat, I think for a while, pondering my choice of song. For some reason, I'm nervous, more nervous than taking the stage at the local bar, more nervous than singing in church. But when I open my mouth, a song comes out. 'La vie en rose'. A song about life through rose-colored glasses, much like the ones I know I'm wearing now.

"That was beautiful," he whispers reverently. "You are…Your voice is…" He pauses. "You're amazing. What is the name of the song?"

I'm surprised he hasn't heard it before. No one should go through life without knowing the songs of Edith Piaf.

"You've never heard it? It's called 'La vie en rose'."

He repeats the words, though his pronunciation is clumsy. I can't help but smile.

"It's French. It means life in pink."

"Life in pink," he says, repeating my words again.

"It's kind of like the phrase seeing life through rose-colored glasses. Everything is cheerful and rosy, tainted with pink." I wonder if he gets the symbolism.

We're silent for a while and then he asks about my friends. So I tell him about Roxy, and the friendship we've shared since going on the date with her brother. I think back to the jealousy and admiration I felt when I first got to know her. She's traveled and seen the world. She speaks of faraway places with a dismissive tone when I can only dream about them. Roxy is everything I wish I could be. Bold and confident. Fearless and worldly. My life felt so small in comparison to hers, but now, I only feel guilt for those feelings. My life before seems so large and bold now that I'm facing a life at the mercy of my requestor.

Looking over at Ryker hesitantly, I ask him about the one thing that's constantly on my mind.

"Tell me about him."

His body tenses, the rose-colored glasses falling from his eyes and shattering on the ground. "You know I can't do that."

"No," I say with firmness. "You can't tell me who he is. I'm not asking for his name. Just tell me about him. He's the son of the man who saved you. Surely he can't be pure evil."

He doesn't say anything and instead stares at the blanket as though it suddenly holds a fascination he wasn't aware of before.

"Tell me."

He doesn't want to, it's plain to see in his expression, but he speaks anyway.

"His father has always been kind to me. Firm but kind. I would hope he would be the same."

My heart falls. "You'd hope?"

Suddenly I understand his interest in the blanket. I trace the diamond pattern of the stars on his shoulders into the weave, wishing and hoping for him to understand my need to know about the man who claims he owns me.

"I know it's strange, asking about him, wanting to know about him when we're caught in this…caught in whatever we are caught in, this pink bubble, but somehow, talking about him makes him less of a monster. If I try to think of him as a person and not the devil merely disguised as one, it helps."

He clears his throat, glancing over at the tray of food. "I forgot something," he says before disappearing out the door.

He's gone a long time, so after waiting for a while, I get up and head to the bathroom, intending to have a shower before he returns.

I don't need the water scalding hot this time. I don't need it to burn my skin and take away the feeling of him. Stepping under the steady stream, I let the water pour over me, finding myself singing the song again. I almost laugh at the absurdity of it. How can I feel happy here? With him? There's a part within me that's screaming, telling me these feelings aren't true, that they are merely a product of my situation. But I don't listen. It feels so good to be happy, to not worry, even if it's only for a moment.

The scent of cherry blossom fills the air as I lather my hair into a bubbly mess and then let the water wash it all out again. Stepping out of the shower, I rub a towel over my hair then wrap it around my body, tucking it over my chest and wearing it like a dress. When I walk back into the room, the light of the camera is back on. Staring at it curiously, I sit on the bed, waiting for Ryker's return.

The door opens with that hushed sound, but instead of the dread I used to feel, I get to my feet, ready to run over and throw myself at him. But he utters those words before he's even through the door, his voice angry and harsh, and tinged with fear.

"Don't say a word."

Without a second thought, I drop to my knees, conditioned to his commands. His eyes are wide and desperate as he stalks toward me.

"Head down," he whispers.

I drop my eyes, that familiar feeling of uncertainty knotting in my chest. Ryker walks behind me, his movements decided and sure. Pulling something out of his pocket, he wraps it over my eyes, covering my vision. It's soft and silky, as though it's made of satin. The material crosses over my ears, amplifying the thud of my heart and muffling his voice, even though his mouth is close to my ear.

"He is here. Keep calm. Just obey."

My heart pounds faster and my skin prickles as dread washes over me. Footsteps echo over the concrete floor.

More than one person. I try to pick who they might be by the sound, but the sounds are nothing more than empty steps over the concrete. I try to inhale their scent, but I can smell nothing but Ryker.

"She's healing well," a deep voice says. Then it drops lower and quieter, muttering words I can't hear. I strain, trying to overhear the conversation but it's pointless. The fabric covering my ears muffles their voices.

A finger slides over my shoulder and I jump, startled by the touch. Then the towel is yanked away, leaving me naked.

"She's marked." This voice has a hysterical lilt to it, like the owner is struggling for control. "She's all broken."

The deep voice speaks again. "We can get you another one, if you like."

"Another?" The voice rises in pitch. "I don't want another! I want my songbird."

Fear lodges itself in my throat. The voice belongs to my requestor. There's something almost childlike about it. And also something familiar. Faces and voices crash through my mind, trying to locate that whiff of recognition. But it is pointless. The voices are too muffled by the blindfold, or I'm too panicked to think clearly.

My head tilts toward Ryker. I can sense him. It's as though there's an aura around him that radiates a heat that only I can feel. There's an echo of a step as someone comes closer.

"Get her to do something." The voice has calmed, but now it holds a hint of excitement, anticipation.

Ryker clears his throat. "Crawl."

"It's my pleasure to obey your command," I utter robotically and drop to my hands and knees, crawling around the room, hoping I don't bump into anything or anyone.

"Stop," Ryker says, and I freeze, awaiting his next command. "Kneel."

Footsteps come toward me, and even without sight or unobstructed sound, I know they don't belong to Ryker. My body tenses, waiting for a foreign touch.

"Open."

My mind races. Open my mouth? Open my legs? It's only a fraction of hesitation but pain slices across my cheek. The force of the blow whips my head back and I sway on my knees, attempting to regain my balance as the pain radiates.

"She didn't obey," my requestor says accusingly.

"What did you want her to open?" Ryker's voice is forced. You can hear the anger caught at the base of this throat.

"May I talk to you a moment? Outside?" the deeper voice says.

No. No. No.

Ryker is leaving.

He's leaving me alone with my requestor.

The door opens and shuts. My heart sinks then beats rapidly, vibrating as though it's caught in the pit of my stomach instead of my chest.

His breath is heavy and sickly sweet, smelling like he'd been drinking nothing but nectar the night before. I can feel it on my skin, warm and thick. He's examining me, pacing in circles like a predator.

"So beautiful," he says and a finger trails over my shoulder. I resist the urge to shudder and will my body not to betray me.

Suddenly his voice is closer, whispered in my ear. "I'm sorry he did that to you, my songbird. But don't worry. He's been taken care of. He'll never be able to lay a finger on you again. He should have known better than to touch what is mine."

I'm trembling now, unable to stop the terror settling in my chest. I want to lash out, yell that I'm not his, but instead I just sit, kneeling in submission as he circles me.

His hand grips my chin, jerking it upward. "My sweet songbird," he hisses in an almost sing-song tone.

And then his tongue is on me, shoving its way into my mouth, more of an attack than a kiss. He moans and grabs my hand from my lap, dragging it upward until I feel his hardness.

"That's all for you, my songbird. When you are mine, I am going to do glorious things to you."

Nausea swells. But then the door opens again and I almost want to cry with relief. The man, whoever he is, steps back from me, letting my hand fall back to my lap.

# CHAPTER FIVE

## MIA

I'm not sure how long I stay kneeling there after they left. I simply sat, waiting for Ryker's return. Waiting for him to come back to me.

But he didn't.

It's dark now. It's been dark for a while. My knees hurt, digging into the cold concrete floor, and my body is cold, frozen almost, though I'm not sure if it's from the temperature alone, or whether the dread that's settled in my stomach has a part to play.

Finally, I move, crawling over to the corner with the chains, pulling my knees to my chest and staring out the window at the stars. It was foolish to allow myself any glimpse of happiness, any shred of hope. I am trapped here. I am a captive. To think anything else is absurd.

The moon is high in the sky when the door finally opens. I don't look up, but I know it's him. Everything about Ryker is familiar to me, from the sound of his steps on the floor to the way he breathes. His feet are bare as he pads over and lowers himself down the wall.

"Are you okay?" Even though spoken softly, the words come out harsh in the stillness of the room.

I don't answer. Instead, I shake my head, allowing a tear to fall. Ryker wipes it away with his thumb, bringing it to his lips and tasting my sadness.

"I didn't know they were coming."

I turn to him then and ask the one thing I've asked so many times before. "Who is he?"

He stares at his hands looped between his knees, then shuffles closer. "You're freezing." Getting to his feet, he walks over to the bed, pulling the blanket away and draping it over me, but I push it aside, not wanting its warmth, its comfort. Not wanting his.

"You'll get sick."

I turn my gaze back to the moon.

"Look at me," he pleads.

And I do. Because that's what I'm here for. To obey. But I keep my expression blank, not wanting to show him the torment that's twisting inside me. He takes my chin gently between his finger and thumb and inches closer, his eyes scanning mine, searching for a hint of... I don't know what. Acceptance? Desire?

He presses his mouth to mine and his lips are hot, almost scalding. His mouth is desperate, but I don't respond. I can't respond. I can't fall into happiness with him again, only to have it ripped from me. It hurts too much.

Ryker tilts his head so our foreheads are pressed together, his breath floating over my face. "Mia, please."

He kisses me again. Desperately. Harshly. Roughly.

"Mia, please," he begs again.

"Please, what?" I say finally. "It would be my pleasure to obey your command."

Those words hit him harder than any physical attack I could have launched. His hands grip into my hair. His storm-filled eyes bore into mine with such intensity I can't keep up this façade of emptiness.

"What do you want from me?" I ask, desperation ripping through my vocal cords. "If you want me to obey, I can do that. If you want to give me over to him, that's your choice. But I can't do this. I can't do us. I can't be trapped in this imitation of happiness only to have it ripped away from me. I'd rather have nothing than have that. Just tell me what you want."

"I want you," Ryker says, his words choked and broken. "I want you free. I want you free to choose me."

"But I am not free. He owns me. He owns my body. You're the one who keeps telling me that. You're the one that made me chant it over and over until the words got stuck in my head." I look straight into his ocean-blue eyes. "There's only one way for me to be free, and that's if you choose it, Ryker. You're the one who holds my freedom in your hands. Just open the door. Let me go."

He pulls away from me, turning back to press his back

against the wall, eyes fixed on the ground. "It's not that simple. I cannot betray them like that. They would kill me. They would kill you. They would kill Everly."

"You've already betrayed them by fucking me."

He blinks at my crassness. "That's different."

"How? Because he doesn't know?" I move to sit in front of him, taking his hands in mine, pleading with him to understand, to be my savior.

"Because he will know. Even though we may never utter a word about our actions, our bodies and our eyes will betray us. Do you not think he will see the longing in my expression if I ever get to see you? And if he ever tries to fuck me—" Ryker winces, flinching as though I have struck him "—he will see your image reflected in my skin. You are burned there. Only you."

Pulling his hands away, he rakes them through his hair. "They know everything about you, Mia. You can't simply walk away and expect there not to be any consequences."

Ignoring his words, I continue to plead with him. "And what about you? Will you be able to see me crawling by his side and not react? Will you be okay with knowing his hands will touch me? His—"

"Enough!" Ryker growls, pushing himself away from me, trying to escape the images I'm forcing into his mind.

"Why? Because that's what's going to happen. He. Will. Know."

"Mia, they know everything about you. Everything. Do

you understand? They know who your parents are. They know your best friend, where she lives, where she works, who she dates. They know the names of your neighbors. They will find you, Mia. There is no doubt about that. There is nothing we can do to escape them. I know what we have is twisted. I know we should stop, that no good can come of this but here, now, us…Being with you is the only part of you I will ever have. I can't stop. I don't want to stop. I crave you. I hate that I crave you, but I do. I'll take any part of you I can get." He grips my face with desperation, pushing his lips against mine with brutality before breaking away again. "I know it is selfish of me, I know I shouldn't be doing this, that I'm only hurting you more, but I can't stop."

He can't stop and I can't resist him. Not now. Not when he's so close, when his lips feel like the only part of heaven I will ever taste. He presses against me until I surrender, lying down on the cold concrete as he crawls over me, pushing his body to mine like he wants to crawl under my skin. His mouth is feverish and desperate, and I lose myself in him until the desire to have him inside me becomes a burning need. An ache of longing so sharp it hurts.

"Please," I moan, unsure what I'm begging for.

"Mia." My name is mumbled by his mouth on my skin.

I need to see him. All of him. I claw at his shirt, peeling it from his body. We detach long enough for it to slip over his head before our mouths collide again. My nails scrape down his back, evoking a glorious groan which falls from his mouth as the pale lines turn red. And then I'm pushing his jeans over his hips, needing him, wanting him. He wrestles himself free, reaching down to tug them from his feet, even as our mouths are still locked in battle. My legs fall open willingly and he pushes inside with one masterful thrust.

I moan. It's a sound filled with pleasure and contentment and want.

He stills, his movements slowing, his mouth becoming lazy and his kisses drawn-out, rather than the feverish desperation of before. I pull him close, not content until every part of us is touching. But he lifts his head back, staring deeply into my eyes as he rocks inside me and pushes a strand of hair back from my face.

"We can't keep doing this." My voice hitches as he pushes deep inside, overwhelming me with pleasure.

"I know," he says.

"It's not safe." I bite my lip, my head tilting backward as the waves of pleasure start to roll.

"I know." His mouth is gentle on the skin of my neck, nibbling and tasting as the tension builds within me. "But I want you," he says. "I need you."

I cry out, whimpers of pleasure echoing off the walls as I convulse under him. They set him off as well and his body tightens over me, muscles straining as an orgasm rips through him, pushing into me harder, deeper, blending our bodies together in a mess of sweat and lust and panting breaths.

Then he rolls off me, chest heaving, an arm thrown over his face as he stares at the ceiling. "Letting you go would be signing your death warrant. I can't do it. I won't do it."

"I know," I say, echoing the same words he used in the throes of passion.

A coldness settles deep in my bones.

I know he will not set me free.

I know I am trapped.

I know this is to be my life.

And I know it is his fault.

"What happened to Marcel?" I roll onto my side to watch him.

He sits up, eyes glancing over at the camera. Panic crosses his expression. "Fuck."

"What happened to Marcel?" I ask again, recalling the words of my requestor.

Ryker gets to his feet, walking toward the door. "He's not here anymore. You don't have to worry about him hurting you. I'll be back in a minute."

I am alone.

Alone and empty.

Alone and cold.

The red light blinks off. Then a few seconds later, it blinks back on again. Getting to my feet, I walk over to the bathroom, stopping in front of the mirror. I stare at my reflection, no longer recognizing the girl who stares back at me.

"You are a captive," I say to her. "He has hurt you and broken you." Taking a deep breath, I stare intently into the mirror, as if trying to convince the girl I see that it is true. "You do not love him."

I can't fool myself any longer.

Walking back into my cell, I sit down on the bed. It's only then I notice the tray of fruit sitting forgotten on the chair in the corner. I notice the apples and the oranges.

I notice the knife.

Almost as though in a trance, I lift myself off the bed and walk over. My finger runs along the blade and a thin red line appears.

Could I do it?

I watch as the blood runs down my finger and drips onto the floor. I imagine holding the blade against Ryker's throat, seeing the confusion and the heartbreak in his eyes.

Could I press it to his skin?

Could I slice the blade and watch him die?

Could I be free?

No. I know I couldn't. But maybe all I'd have to do is threaten him. Would he be willing to risk himself to keep me here?

Squeezing the handle in my fist, I sit back on the bed, tucking the knife under the blanket, and await Ryker's return.

When he walks back in, he is still unclothed and the beauty of him twists in my gut. I blink back the tears and the confusion, knowing what I must do. Knowing I have no choice. If I hold the blade to his neck, he will have to let me go. He will have to wait as I open the door and set myself free.

But what if he doesn't? What if he calls my bluff? Would I be able to follow through on my threat? Would I be able to hurt him in order to free myself? I break out in a sweat just thinking about it. The blood drains from my face and my hands go clammy with the cold.

Upon seeing my distress, Ryker walks over, falling to the space between my legs, kneeling on the ground and looking at me with those storm-filled eyes.

"Don't cry," he says, once again wiping away my tears. "I will figure this out. I will keep you safe."

But safety isn't what I want. Freedom is. I used to think they were the same thing.

My hand trembles as I slide it through the sheets, searching for the cold bluntness of the knife's hidden handle. I'm chanting internally, repeating the only words that can strengthen me, even though they are a lie.

*I do not love him.*

*I do not love him.*

*I do not love him.*

He doesn't notice the knife until the blade is pressed to his throat, and even then, it's only his eyes closing and then opening again slowly that gives me any clue that he understands what I'm about to do.

"You know I can't let you leave." His words are pained.

The movement of this throat as he speaks presses against the blade, drawing the finest line of blood.

"Let me go or I'll use this." I can't even bring myself to call it what it is, and Ryker sees the hesitation in my eyes. He sees the torment and the conflict and presses his throat against the blade further.

"I won't do it, Mia." A single trickle of blood runs down his neck. "I won't let you die. I can't. I'd rather you be with him than dead."

"This time," I say, leaning close to whisper in his ear and ignoring the waves of conflicting emotions crashing through me as I inhale his scent. "You're not the one who gets to choose."

He shakes his head drawing more blood from the friction of the blade. "You won't do it. You can't do it."

"Let me go."

His voice is torn. "No."

A battle rages within, but I think of my mother, my father, of Roxy and all the people in my small town. There is no way Roxy would hesitate over this. She would take the blade and plunge it into him without a thought. She would put herself through hell rather than let someone take over her life. So, I think of the life I want and then I think of the life I will have if I don't do this. Nothing but a plaything for a deranged man. Owned.

It only takes an instant. Just a quick flick of my hand and I plunge the knife into his shoulder. He cries out in pain and falls to the ground, the knife stuck deep into his flesh. The dull thud when I plunged it in makes me think I hit bone. Blood seeps across the floor. Ryker is groaning, though he doesn't move. He just lies there with desperation in his eyes as he stares at me. His lips form my name but no sound comes out.

There's no time to think.

There's no time for remorse.

It's now or never.

Rushing toward the door, I jerk it open, grateful for Ryker's habit of not locking it while he is with me, and find a hallway and an opening with an array of monitors sitting on a desk. On one of them, Ryker lies on the ground. Star is in another. But I tear past the screens, heading for the glimpse of a stairway visible just beyond. I take the stairs two at a time, not caring how much noise I make, desperation for escape the only thing guiding me, and then I burst through the door, both excited and scared of what is on the other side.

But there's nothing but horses faintly outlined by the light of the moon to greet me. They breathe heavily, snorting at my sudden appearance. I spot another door down the far end and sprint, scared that my escape will be thwarted at any second.

Pushing against the wooden door, it breaks open and I am outside. Outside and alone. My heart pounds in my ears. My veins pump panic and hope, tainting my blood.

Then, I run.

Stones cut into my bare feet. Grass lashes against my ankles. But I am free. I keep running through fields and paddocks until I come across a road. In the distance, I see the lights of an approaching car.

Do I wave it down or do I hide?

Fear decides for me as I dive into the grass, hiding from the glare of the lights. What if it's him? What if it is my requester?

The car slows. My heart races. Pulling to a stop, the window of the car rolls down. In the darkness, I can't see the details of his face. I can only see blue eyes. I fight within myself, not knowing whether to stay hidden or whether to hope for the kindness of a stranger.

After waiting a while, the window winds back up, the eyes disappear, and the car pulls back onto the road.

A sob escapes as I get to my feet, turning away from the road and running toward a grove of trees that stand dark and tall in the moonlight. I stumble over sticks and stones that cut into my feet, but I don't notice the pain. I don't notice the whip of the wind as it tosses my hair. I don't notice anything but the sound of my feet on the ground and the thud of my heart.

The fullness of the moon allows me enough light to see where I am going but the desperate panic of my movements cause me to stagger, my hands bracing against the ground, keeping me upright as I race through the trees. A mound of dirt rises beneath me, fresh and loose and I fall face first into its dampness. Scrambling back to my feet, I keep running, my breaths coming out as white fog in the darkness.

I'm not sure how long I run. I'm not sure which direction I'm running in or where I hope to go.

My only thought is escape.

ryker

# CHAPTER SIX

## RYKER

Pulling the shower curtain open, I stare at Marcel's body hunched over the tiles. His gaze is still fixed upward as though he's waiting for my return. Blood has pooled at the bottom of the shower, coagulating into a thick dark puddle. Turning on the showerhead, I wash the deep red stain away, nudging the body away from the drain with my foot. I close his eyes then bend down to heave him over my shoulder.

I do all this but I'm not thinking about it. I shed no tears for this loss of life. It is what it is. He knew the risk he took the moment he walked into her room. Instead, all I can think about is her. The welts over her back. The look of desperation in her eyes as she pleaded with me to let her go. The way she felt trembling against me. The heat of her body. The softness of her lips.

The narrow stairs are hard to maneuver with Marcel hoisted over my shoulder. I keep bumping into the walls, cursing when his leg or his hand bang noisily.

There's a small patch of forest out the back of the stables.

I dig by the light of the moon, not wanting to create any attention with a flashlight. The ground is cold but soft. The roots of the trees are the only resistance. Something flutters and lands on a branch above me, watching my movements in the dim light. I feel like it is judging me, cocking its head side to side as though warning of some sort of evil to come. After a while, I throw a stick in its direction, watching as it takes flight and disappears into the darkness of the night.

When the hole is large enough and deep enough, I push Marcel's body into it, letting it fall to the bottom in a crumpled pile. I'm tempted to jump in, leave him in a more comfortable position for the afterlife, but then the image of him wrapped around Mia with ravenous lust rising off him like steam jumps to the front of my mind, and I dump dirt over him until there's nothing left but a dark mound rising above the level of the ground.

The horses whinny when I walk back into the stables, shaking their heads as if they know what I've done. I pat the one I've come to call Blaze and press my forehead to her, uttering words that only she can hear. I tell her about what he did. And about what I almost did. Of how I pressed my lips to hers and wanted to do so much more, even while she was still broken and bruised. I told her of my conflict. My desire to set Mia free. Blaze reels back at my confession, shaking her head and stomping her feet.

"I know, I know," I mutter. "There would be another mound in the ground if I let her go, you don't think I know that?"

She snorts, blowing hot air over my face.

"Yes, I agree. I need to make her understand. I just don't know how." The horse snickers then whinnies again, tossing its mane. Some of the other horses join in as if to lend their support.

When I first arrived at the Atterton residence, the horses frightened me. I was young and malnourished from my life on the streets. That was before Mr Atterton found me. I don't remember a lot about my childhood, and what I do remember, I want to forget. He took me and my sister in. He looked after us both. He fed us, housed us and educated us. I hate to think of what our lives would have been without him. In no small manner, I owe him my life. My loyalty and my obedience guarantee my sister's safety. It guarantees her life free from the underbelly of existence that I have been thrust into. But it is worth it to keep her safe. It is worth it for Everly to have choices, the ability to make something of herself and be someone I could never hope to be. It's a sacrifice I would make time and time again. But to explain that to Mia would be almost impossible.

How could she understand that the man who stole her is the man who saved me?

The morning has just broken when the sounds of the tires on the doctor's car crunch over the gravel. I lead him down the stairs and key in the code to Mia's door. I can't even look at her when we enter but I know she's looking at me. I feel the weight of her gaze. And the guilt it brings burns. Everything that has happened to her is my fault. Maybe not directly, but I am the one keeping her here. I am the one ensuring her captivity. The doctor performs his examination as I stand sullenly in the corner, arms crossed over my chest and doing my best not to show the weakness that resides within. The weakness that longs to pick her up and carry her away from this place, despite the consequences I know it will bring. That is why I can't look at her. Because if I do, the temptation will be too much.

But when he asks me to hold her in place, I can't help it. Her eyes are filled with confusion and she looks at me with need. But I don't deserve to be looked at like that. Not by her. She deserves so much more. I have nothing to offer. And I don't tell her what the injection is for because I don't want to think about it.

She calls out to me when I leave. Her voice is as soft as a whisper and at first, I think I imagine it, I think it is my mind playing tricks on me by fooling me with words I long to hear. But then she speaks again, and I know the words to be real. She begs me to look at her, but I can't do it again. I'm not that strong.

Following the doctor out the door, I wait and listen as he gives me the instructions for her care. "And because of where she is in her cycle, you will need to wait seven days before any sexual intercourse. I'll have the results of all her blood tests back shortly and I'm sure Mr Atterton will keep you informed. I don't anticipate any need to see her again until her injection is due in around twelve weeks."

I escort him out and watch until his car disappears into the distance.

Walking back down the stairs, I dump myself in front of the monitors, my eyes flicking from screen to screen. All the girls are motionless, staring blankly at walls or out the small square of a window. Mia has her back to the camera. The sheet has fallen down her side, exposing the angry red welts. She needs the cream applied. But I can't be the one to do it. I'm afraid of my reaction, of the conflicted torment that's raging inside me. Is it possible to want to protect and devour something at the same time?

Gathering creams and cloths and bandages from the collection the doctor left, I load them onto a tray. Then, on second thought, I pop into the kitchen and grab a few pieces of fruit. She will need to keep her strength up. When I push open the door to Star's cell, she immediately stands, running over to fall at my feet.

"Get up," I say harshly.

"Yes, Master." She gets to her feet, but still has this submissive stance, one that reminds me of Marcel.

"Don't call me that."

"Yes, Mas—" Her head drops further. "Yes." And then she glances up quickly, but not at me, she glances over to the door.

"He's not coming." Disappointment slumps her

shoulders. I don't understand it. I saw Marcel treat her with nothing but cruelty and contempt but here she is, mourning the loss of him.

"Is he okay?" Her voice is so faint I have to strain to hear it.

"He's been transferred."

Sadness prickles her skin and her eyes well with tears.

"I'll be taking over until your new trainer arrives." She nods. "But first, I need your help with something."

"Yes, Mas—" She nods again.

"The girl in the cell next to you has been hurt. I need someone to look after her, clean her wounds." I shove the tray at her. "Come with me."

She follows obediently, eyes kept on the ground even as I walk her out the door. I expect her to look around with curiosity, but she doesn't.

"Here." I stop at Mia's door. "Make sure she eats." And then I add, "And be gentle."

I return to my seat to watch them. Mia's lips move so I turn up the volume, wanting to hear what they are talking about, but their voices are too quiet, their words too mumbled. But Star does as I've instructed. She cleans her wounds. She makes sure Mia eats. And once she is done, she heads back to her cell under my watch, but there's a question in her eyes.

"Will he come back?" she asks.

I shake my head, not wanting to say the words out loud

because I know, for some fucked up reason, they will break her heart. But now is the time she chooses to display a fragment of defiance.

"I want to see him."

"You can't." I turn to walk away, but she grabs me, pulling on my shirt.

"Please," she begs, falling to her knees. "I need to see him."

"He's gone."

She latches onto my foot like a child unwilling to let go of its mother and starts wailing uncontrollably. Her eyes are filled with tears of desperation. So I speak to her in the language she's been trained to understand and slap her across the face.

"Silence!" I order.

The effect is immediate. Her crying stops. Her tears dry. She lets go of my legs and kneels in a position of submission.

"Yes, Master."

I walk out of her cell and slump onto the chair in front of the monitors. The guilt of what I've become weighs heavily. I need to remind myself why I'm doing it, so I pull my cell out of the drawer and dial the familiar number.

"Ryker!" her voice is cheerful and happy, a breath of fresh air.

"Hey, sis."

A request for video calling appears on the screen. "Turn it on," her voice demands teasingly.

I do and the image of my sister appears. She must have come straight from some sort of practice as she's still in shorts and a t-shirt, a scarf wrapped around her neck the only thing keeping her warm. She looks pale. She looks thin, as though she's lost weight.

"Have you been eating?"

She rolls her eyes, sitting herself down on the couch of her apartment. An apartment paid for by the Attertons. A couch paid for by the Attertons.

"I'm fine," she insists, tucking an ankle under her knee and snuggling back into the cushions. Reaching out of frame, her hand appears again with a packet of biscuits. The ones with pale pink icing and sprinkled with colorful sugar beads. The ones I sent her in a package three weeks ago.

"See?" she says, opening the packet. There's only two left. Putting the packet down beside her, she looks straight at me, a slight frown creasing her brow. "Where are you?" Her eyes float around the screen, trying to discern the background.

"Nowhere," I lie. "I'm on a job."

Her frown deepens. "You look sad. Is everything okay?"

I sigh. "I'm fine. Everything is fine. I just needed to hear your voice. Make sure you're okay."

"Of course I'm okay, silly. You need to stop worrying about me. Life is wonderful." She smiles brilliantly as if it proves her point. "The teachers here are amazing. I'm learning so much."

I roll my eyes at her forced enthusiasm. "I hope you're

taking this seri—"

"My god, Ryker," Everly says, exasperated. "Would you stop worrying for one second? Just be happy. Be happy I'm here. Be happy I'm learning and making all those stupid connections you say are good for me."

"I am," I insist.

There's a ruckus in the background, the sound of opening doors and giggling voices. Everly looks up, smiling at whoever just entered her apartment. "I've got to go," she says. "Look after yourself and stop worrying!"

And then she's gone, and I am left alone with my thoughts again.

Over the next few days, I send Star in to tend Mia's wounds. I can't face her knowing that the reason this happened is because I couldn't protect her. And I still can't protect her. She is to be Junior's, not mine. I have no right to feel the way I do. So instead, I watch her on the monitor like some sick fuck getting his rocks off. I watch each of the girls, but mainly, I watch Mia. Her eyes often flick to the camera, as though she knows I'm here. At times, I imagine her calling my name, desperate for my touch. Other times, I imagine her turning away from me in disgust, knowing what I did, what I am capable of.

And at night the nightmares have begun again. It's been years since I've had them, but suddenly, I've found myself waking in the middle of the night, cold sweat drenching both my body and the sheets beneath me, my heart pounding against my chest like a hammer. It's only when I look up and see her still there, safe in her bed that my panic starts to subside. I used to get them when I was younger. I would wake almost paralyzed with fear, only to have no idea what I'd dreamed. I only had the memory of the emotion of the dream, not the details. It is the same now. I don't know what it is I'm dreaming about, I only know the terror in which I wake.

I've started drinking more so I fall to sleep in a blissful state of oblivion, but it only lasts so long, and my dreams are too sobering for it to have any real effect.

By the fifth day, I am a wreck. I haven't washed or eaten anything in days. My breath stinks of whiskey, my bedding reeks of me. And I have become desperate to see her. Like some sort of freak, I stroke the screen as I watch her, as though I can feel her skin under my fingertips, soft and smooth.

I need a distraction.

Rummaging through the drawers, I find my cell phone and plug it in. There are no missed calls. Not even from Everly. She doesn't call often, too wrapped up in her own life to be worried about mine, and that's the way it should be.

Shuffling through my limited contacts I come across the number I want. I need something to take my mind off Mia.

She's consumed me. I can't get her out of my mind. Being trapped here with her is torture, or denied pleasure, or a combination of both. And since whiskey doesn't seem to be doing the job, there's only one option left.

"Hey, big boy," a soft voice purrs. "Long time no see."

I clear my throat, suddenly uncomfortable. "Hey, Angel. Yeah, it's been a while." Months in fact. Angel was just someone I used when the loneliness got a little too much.

"You wanting some company?"

"Sort of. Only, I'm not in the city. So, I was wondering if…" my voice fades. It is a stupid idea. As though phone sex is going to be able to take my mind off what is waiting in the cell across the hall. "Look, forget it, okay? I made a mistake."

I hang up, throwing my cell phone back into the drawer and slamming it shut. It starts ringing again almost immediately, but I ignore it. I know there's only one way I'm going to be able to get this longing out of my system, this need to have her look at me, a look which isn't filled with disappointment.

I need to make her understand. I need her to know the truth and not stare at me with that pleading desperation in her eyes. Pushing my way into the bathroom, I turn on the shower, doing my best not to look down at where he lay. Not to think about what I did, what the same hands that I want to caress her skin with are capable of.

I lather my hair into a mess and turn the water to scalding

hot, as though it will wash away the memory of his blood. I've killed before so it's not the actual act that haunts me, it's the knowledge of her finding out. Of her looking into my eyes and knowing that I am no better than the man who requested her.

In fact, I may be worse.

# CHAPTER SEVEN

## RYKER

Fuck.

I am fucked.

The moment I walk into her cell, she falls to her knees. I run my finger down the soft skin of her cheek and that's when I know it. I know I am fucked because I cannot resist her. I can't fight the urge to press my lips to her skin. But not in a way I've been instructed to. Not in a way that conditions her to touch, that teaches her to accept her fate. In a way that is filled with lust and longing. In a way that will quench the need I see in her eyes.

I've been aching for her to look at me that way, and now that she is, all I can think of are the ways I don't deserve it.

The way I stripped her.

The way I chained her.

The way I demanded her obedience.

Killed for her.

She thinks I'm angry, she even asks me. Her voice quivers like the thought of me being angry would be too much to bear. How little she knows. I need to make her understand.

So I tell her how I can't free her. I can't betray them. I try to make her understand my enforced loyalty to the family and how, despite the way I feel about her, there is no escape.

Once I am done, once my heart has been wrenched out and thrown at her feet, she lifts a trembling hand, reaching out to touch my face. I inhale deeply, knowing what her touch will do to me. Knowing that I am going to let her. She cups my cheeks, bringing her mouth closer and closer until her lips brush against mine. It is the softest and most powerful kiss I've ever felt. It sets off a torrent of emotions fighting for dominance. Lust. Despair. Longing. Torment.

Then she cups my face fully, kissing me more passionately, more deeply, tugging at the knot of desire twisted in my gut until I can't contain it anymore and push my fingers through her hair, pulling her closer, wanting her, needing her. But I want to show her that I'm not like them. I do not want her submissive and silent. I do not want her succumbing to me because she has no choice.

I want her to want me.

To need me.

To crave me.

Pulling away, I drop to my knees at her feet, offering myself in submission in the same way I have demanded of her all those times before. She bends to kiss me again, locking my bottom lip between her teeth and tugging in such a way the pain shoots straight to my cock, hardening it even further. Lowering herself onto my lap, she tears off my shirt, running her fingers over my skin. It feels like heaven to have her finally touching me, no walls, no rules between us.

As if trying to crawl under my skin, she pushes me to the ground, grinding on top of me like a sinful goddess. She becomes desperate, tugging my belt away and ripping off my jeans. And then she stands, slowly slipping her dress over her body, leaving her naked and exposed. And even though I've seen her naked many times before, it's never been like this. It's never been openly, willingly.

A moan fills the air and I'm surprised to realize that it came from me. She is starkly beautiful, even with the welts and dark patches covering her skin. Somehow, they almost make her more beautiful, but it is a beauty etched with sadness and regret for what I allowed him to do.

Every part of me is tight and taut with hunger for her. I want to take her, press her against the wall and fuck her until she cries out my name. But instead, I push the urge down, denying myself that pleasure until she asks for it. Until she begs.

Fingers lock around my ankles and travel up my legs, digging into my flesh in agonizing bliss. She touches every part of me until I am the one who wants to beg. I need to be inside her. I need to feel her tightness clamped around me, pulsing with undenied ecstasy.

But she doesn't make me beg. She lowers herself onto me slowly, allowing me to feel everything, every fraction of movement, every throb and quiver. It's only then that she reaches for my hands, bringing them to her hips, allowing me to guide our movements. I dig my fingers into her flesh, leaving imprints.

I need more.

Lifting myself from the ground, I want to feel her skin under my tongue, mold her flesh with my hands, but she pushes me back down forcefully, her hand pressed to my chest as she lifts and then lowers herself, riding me.

Her hand creeps up my chest, wrapping around my neck, squeezing until the tightness cuts off my air, making me lightheaded. But I don't stop her or pull her hand away. I'm caught in some exquisite state of rapture. And when she does release me, my hand snakes out and snaps around her wrist, almost of its own accord.

She slaps me.

I convulse, an orgasm so close, just on the brink.

And then she says something that pushes it closer, nearly undoing me.

"Take me."

Thought and control leave, and I lift her, twisting her beneath me and sinking into her as her legs wrap around my waist. Our movements become blurred with passion, feverish with desire. I'm ravenous, writhing against her, devouring her. It's only when I feel her lose herself to me that I still, watching her expression as wave after wave of pleasure rips through her body. The way the flush of red kisses her cheeks. The way she bites her lip before she cries out my name.

I lazily kiss those fuckable lips as a smile creeps over her face.

It takes all my willpower to withdraw. Every ounce I have. But I can't stay inside her. I can't risk her future.

"What are you doing?" Her hands grip my ass cheeks, holding me firmly within her. "What about you?"

"This isn't about me."

Her mouth moves to lick the skin just below my ear. My cock surges once again as she bites and pushes herself onto me further, making it torture for me to pull out.

"No protection," I grunt.

She blinks a few times, as if considering her options and I take the opportunity to detangle myself from her, drawing in a deep breath and trying to calm the part of me that is screaming to plunge inside her again and fuck her relentlessly until I shatter.

She lowers herself to her knees to take me in her mouth, but I stop her, not wanting any part of this to reflect on what we've done before. What I've demanded of her before.

"Not on your knees," I say, pulling her to her feet.

No sooner are the words out of my mouth that she launches herself at me, wrapping her legs around my waist, pushing her wetness against my hardness once more.

Powerless against her, I groan and enter her again.

My willpower is draining. I walk backward, pressing my

back to the wall and I slip my hands under the cheeks of her ass, sliding her up and down on my cock until the sensation is too much and I toss her onto the bed, clutching myself as her body trembles, the movement swaying her breasts. Grabbing her ankles, I pull her toward me, wanting to taste her. She tastes of cherry blossoms and lemon. Sweet and tangy.

She calls out my name when she comes again, and it is everything I've been dreaming of, so I whisper that as I crawl back over her body, relishing the look of utter bliss on her face. She reaches between us, taking me in her hands and working me up and down until I can't resist anymore. I spurt over her stomach and slump over her, spreading the slickness of me over both our bodies.

Her skin burns beneath mine. Her breasts push against my chest, rising and falling with each breath. Her fingers trace over my skin making it skittish.

"How did you get this?" she asks when she finds my scar.

Reality comes crashing back. "It's nothing," I say, sitting up, blocking the memory from my mind. It's a truth she doesn't need to know. I don't want to think about the world beyond these walls. I don't want to think about the fate that awaits her. I want to distract myself with her, because this right here, right now, is the only part of her I'm ever going to have.

I take her in the shower.

I wake with her sprawled across me and I take her again.

And then I lie, wrapped in her until the sun is halfway across the sky. It's not until I think about what we've done that fear spikes within me. I failed to withdraw and came deep inside her. The doctor's words run through my mind.

*Seven days.*

It's only been six.

I am a selfish and stupid man. But when I tell her it's like she doesn't care, or doesn't want to know, because she almost turns away from me, and denies my offer of bringing back the doctor. Even before the words are out of my mouth, I know they are a lie. There is no way I could bring the doctor back here for this reason. Senior would know and then Mia and Everly would be at risk. But I can't let her see my fear so I scramble for an excuse to leave and gather my thoughts. My stomach reminds me it's been a long time since I've eaten. But first off, I need coffee.

"You want coffee?" I ask.

The excitement in her eyes over something so small kills me.

"Coffee? I would die for some coffee," she says dreamily, lying back on the bed, her eyes raking over me hungrily and making me want this moment to last forever.

Grabbing my jeans, I tug them over my legs and then reach for my t-shirt. But Mia leans off the bed, grabbing it and jerking it away from me. She shakes her head with a wicked grin and laughs, twisting on the bed as though she doesn't have a care in the world.

This is who she is.

This is the girl I have a part in ruining.

As I make the coffee, listening to the gurgle and whir of the coffee machine, I try not to think of the consequences of my mistake. I curse myself for my stupidity, for putting hers and Everly's lives at risk for the rapture of a few moments. After quickly checking on the other girls via the monitors, I also grab a few pieces of fruit and the knife and load them onto the tray for breakfast.

Mia has taken the blanket off the bed and laid it on the floor as though we are about to have a picnic. Placing the tray on the seat in the corner, I hand her one of the coffees and grab the other for myself, lowering myself on the blanket next to her.

With the burn of lust in my veins temporarily sated, I look over at her, wanting to know every part of her life, every detail of what makes her who she is.

"Now that I've told you about my sorry excuse of a childhood, tell me about yours. What's your mother like? Your father?"

Of course, I already know the answers to these questions, but I don't want to know what is written in some file. I want to know from her. To hear her voice.

She takes a sip of the coffee and her eyes roll back in rapture. "Oh my god," she groans. "I had forgotten what sweet nectar this is." She takes another sip and groans again.

My cock twitches, mistaking her moans for ones of a

different kind.

She looks up at me with those big dark eyes I have gotten lost in all too often. "There's not a lot to tell, really. My parents are still together, stupidly in love." She grins and lies back onto the blanket, one ankle coming to rest over the knee bent in the air. "They own a bakery." She shrugs. "There's not a lot else to tell really. I mainly keep to myself."

I know she's not telling the truth. Well, not all of it anyway, but I don't begrudge her that. She's right to hide parts of herself from me. I don't deserve to know her truth.

"Surely there must be more to your life than your parents?" I prompt, just wanting to hear the sound of her voice while it's happy and carefree and not told to be silent.

She shrugs. "You probably know everything anyway."

I shake my head.

"Well," she thinks for a while, chewing on her bottom lip. "I sing a little. Sometimes." She shifts on the blanket, smiling at me shyly.

"Would you sing for me?"

"Here?"

I can't help the smile that creeps across my face. "Yes, here."

She fidgets with the edge of the blanket nervously and looks up at me through long dark lashes that ignite a different sort of desire than wanting to hear her sing. I hold my breath, waiting for her answer. She's quiet for so long, I think she's going to refuse my request. But then she opens her mouth and starts to sing.

Goosebumps prickle my skin.

Her voice is so sweet, so delicate, as if no evil could exist in the world. Her dark eyes look at me coyly, her voice growing stronger and more confident the more she sings. I'm ashamed to say I don't know the song. Parts of the song are in a language I don't understand but the melody is beautiful and soulful, reminding me of the world she lives in. A world that isn't mine. A happy world. Carefree and sweet.

When she finishes, she smiles nervously, as though worried what I think.

"That was beautiful," I whisper reverently. "You are…Your voice is…" my voice breaks away, overwhelmed with a sadness so sweet it hurts. "You're amazing."

"I'm not really."

"Yes, you are." I shuffle closer. "What is the name of the song?"

"You've never heard it?" She seems surprised, as though everyone should know it. "La vie en rose."

I repeat the words, unsure of the pronunciation.

"It's French," she says. "It means life in pink."

"Life in pink," I mimic. It's like she's speaking a different language herself. The concept of music like this is foreign to me. My playlists consist of metal and rock, meant to feed the rage inside me.

"It's kind of like the phrase 'seeing life through rose-colored glasses'. Everything is cheerful and rosy, tainted with pink."

We let silence fall as the contradiction of the song and the world we've found ourselves in clashes in our minds. Her smile fades and everything within me just wants to see it again.

"Tell me about your friends," I prompt, just wanting to hear her voice again.

"Roxy," she says and I think of the girl with the pixie-cut hair confronting me outside her house.

She screws up her face and laughs, recalling memories I'm not privy to. "She's like the complete opposite of me in every way possible. She's blonde, I'm brunette. She's short, I'm tall. She hates spicy food, I love it. She's into country music and I tell her I despise it, but that's more to piss her off than anything else. Really, I don't mind it all that much."

This is how she must have been before. Happy. Carefree. Fucking gorgeous.

She talks for a long time and I'm content just to listen to the sound of her voice. It has a musical quality about it, a gentle laughter hidden beneath her tone that I've never heard before. But of course, that's because she's never had the chance.

After a while, she turns onto her side, looking up at me through dark lashes. "Tell me about him."

The walls start closing in. "You know I can't do that."

"No. You can't tell me who he is. I'm not asking for his name. Just tell me about him. He's the son of the man who saved you. Surely he can't be pure evil."

I don't know how to answer. How can I tell her that when I look into his eyes, I only see darkness?

"Tell me," she urges again.

"His father has always been kind to me. Firm but kind. I would hope he would be the same."

"You'd hope?"

I nod, letting my eyes fall to the ground and swallow the knot of lies waiting in the base of my throat. She traces a pattern on the blanket with her finger and I recall how it felt when she first did it to the ink over my shoulder.

"I know it's strange, asking about him, wanting to know about him when we're caught in this…" She pauses for a moment, struggling to find the right word. "Caught in whatever we are caught in, this pink bubble, but somehow, talking about him makes him less of a monster. If I try to think of him as a person and not this devil merely disguised as one, it helps."

I want to reassure her. Tell her that everything will be okay, but I know it would be a lie.

I glance over at the tray of food, needing an excuse to escape and gather my thoughts. "I've forgotten something," I say, getting to my feet. "Back in a moment."

# CHAPTER EIGHT

## RYKER

Senior and Junior are standing by the monitors. Senior's arms are crossed, his brows pressed into a firm line. I try not to let the surprise and the panic show on my face. What are they doing here?

"Why are they switched off?" Senior lifts one brow in question, then allows his eyes to move down to my bare chest, lifting that brow even higher.

My heart pounds with alarm but I do my best to school my features into a scowl. "I got sick of fucking looking at them," I reply grumpily, hoping my annoyance will distract from my shirtless and tousled appearance. "What are you doing here anyway?" I flick the monitors back on, praying that Mia behaves accordingly. She won't know they're out here. She's still lying on the blanket in the middle of the floor, her hands lifted as though they are dancing with the air. She lies like that for a while, completely unaware of the eyes watching her. I inwardly beg for her to look over at the camera and see the blinking red light, but instead, she gets to her feet, her perfect ass disappearing into the bathroom.

"You fucking let him put his hands on her," Junior spits the words out. He's not concerned about her injuries, in fact, the way his eyes gleam as they fix on her back, on the welts across her upper thighs, I think they excite him.

Mia steps under the water, lathering her hair. She turns, her face visible to the camera, and smiles. Her mouth is moving and Junior leans in to turn up the volume. Her voice is only just audible over the hum of the shower and his face pales.

"I thought I instructed she was to be trained in silence. What the fuck is she doing singing?"

I shift uncomfortably as Senior's eyes burn into the side of my head, but I pretend not to notice his glare. Beside me, Junior quivers, his body shaking with rage.

"Is she going to heal okay? I want her skin fucking flawless. No bruising. No cuts or marks. Just a blank canvas."

A shudder erupts at his words. A blank canvas implies he doesn't want to keep it that way.

Junior rubs his hands together as she steps out of the shower. Wet and glistening, she's never looked so beautiful. It's like her skin glimmers under the light, defying the dark bruises that stain it. Her hair, dark and in wet strands, drapes around her shoulders and falls to where the towel is wrapped around her. She steps out of the bathroom and her eyes flick up to the camera, a small frown pressing between her brows as she sits on the edge of the bed.

"We're here to inspect her," Senior says.

"She's not ready," I say hastily, and then try to backtrack as suspicion lifts Senior's brow again. "Marcel's interference set us back a few steps."

Junior, now with his hands pressed like a prayer beneath his chin, watches her intently. "I want to see her."

Senior pats him on the back. "And you shall." He directs a warning glare my way. "Get her ready. We would like a demonstration of your progress to date. I'm sure she's capable of obeying specific commands."

Junior closes his eyes, breathing deeply. "Make sure she's blindfolded. I don't want to ruin the surprise just yet."

I'm not sure what he expects of her when she finds out who he is. Does he think she'll run into his arms? Fall at his knees and beg him to fuck her?

Digging into his pocket, he pulls out a piece of fabric. "Here, use this."

I clear my throat, scrambling through my mind for an excuse to stop them. But there is nothing. They own her. They own me. I wave the strip of material pathetically.

"I'll go get her ready."

Fortunately, neither of them notice that I don't have to key in a code to unlock the door. I take a deep breath as I walk in, uttering the command phrase harshly before I even see her. My heart sighs in relief when she drops to her knees, but she looks up at me questioningly.

"Head down," I whisper, walking behind her to wrap the material over her eyes. "He is here. Just obey."

Her body tenses at my words. Goosebumps erupt over her skin and for the briefest of moments, I am distracted, wishing I could soothe them with my tongue.

Senior and Junior walk into the small room. It's crowded with them in here, suffocating. Junior's eyes are fixed firmly on Mia. I can almost see the drool forming at the corners of his mouth.

Senior inspects her as one might a vehicle, or a horse, or any other thing they might wish to purchase. He bends down, studying the welts on her back.

"She is healing well." His eyes roam over her body hungrily. "She will fit in well with the others."

"The others?"

"Dad thinks she will be joining his little collection." Junior's eyes flash in anger as he glares at his father. "She won't."

Senior rolls his eyes. "Everything is all set up there. She would be hap—"

But Junior holds up a hand, silencing Senior as he steps toward Mia, walking around her like his father did previously. When he reaches out to touch her shoulder, she flinches. Junior's eyes jump with excitement and he wrenches the towel away from her, leaving her naked.

"She's marked," he says with disgust. "She's all broken."

There's something about his tone which implies it's my

fault. He is digging for a rise, almost begging for me to punch him. Instead, I smile grimly.

"We can get you another one, if you like," Senior says.

"Another? I don't want another. She is mine. I want my songbird."

I grit my teeth and hope the bulge of my jaw isn't obvious.

"Get her to do something," Junior demands.

Everything within me wants to barrel into Junior, push his shoulders into the wall and press my arm across his throat. But thoughts of Everly, and thoughts of what punishment he would dole out to Mia are the only things that stop me.

"Crawl," I command, pushing as much authority into my voice as I can muster.

"It's my pleasure to obey your command." Her voice is small and trembles with fear. There's no hint of the musical laughter that threaded through its tone only moments before.

She drops to her knees and begins to crawl blindly around the room. Junior follows her every moment with beady eyes. She's about to crawl straight into the wall so I command her to stop and kneel. Junior almost looks disappointed. He stalks toward her with a ravenous hunger in his eyes.

"Open," he commands.

Mia's head tilts toward me, knowing where I am from the sound of my voice. There's hesitation in her stance and Junior's hand shoots out and whacks her across her face, the force of it whipping her head to the side and creating a trickle of blood as one of her wounds reopens. It takes everything within me not to run to her, not to attack Junior.

He looks at me accusingly. "She didn't obey."

Clenching my teeth until they hurt, I speak through withheld aggression. "What did you want her to open?"

Senior's words cut through the tension before Junior can answer. "May I talk to you a moment." Even though it is phrased like one, I know it's not a request. "Outside," he adds.

It takes all my willpower to look away from Mia. She's in the room alone with Junior. It's all I can think about as I follow Senior out the door. My eyes immediately lock on the monitor, watching Junior as he stalks around her, pacing in a circle, trailing his finger over her skin.

Senior clears his throat, head cocked to the side, waiting for me to meet his eye.

"You wanted to talk?" I say, forcing myself not to look back at the screen.

"The girl hasn't been broken yet."

"She didn't know what he wanted her to open. This was his fault, not hers."

"I'm not talking about that. I'm talking about the way she listens and reacts. You've trained her well if her purpose is for her to pretend to obey, but it's not. It needs to be real. It's the only way this girl will survive."

Senior's studying me intently as if searching for something hidden in my eyes. All I want to do is look at the screen, make sure she is okay.

"I told you I had no experience with—"

Senior holds up a hand. "Don't lie to me."

"I'm not lying. I'm trying to ex—"

He steps so close I stop speaking, his face hovering only inches away from mine. Even though he is shorter than me, there is something predatory in his gaze.

"Your poker face is slipping," he hisses. "You couldn't hide your emotion when he punished her. It took everything within you not to lash out, didn't it?" Do I need to be worried, Ryker? Just remember, a betrayal of my son is a betrayal of me. I will do what I can to protect the girl, but you need to help me." He turns away, walking toward the steps that lead upstairs. "Tell my son I will meet him in the car." He climbs up the first two stairs, throwing a comment behind him. "You can look at the screen now."

I keep my gaze fixed on him as we glare at each other. Senior finally pulls his away and carries on walking up the stairs. I wait to hear ten of his clipped steps before darting my eyes back to Mia.

Junior is bent low, whispering in her ear. Her body is held taut, as though she's ready to leap away as soon as she's given the chance.

"And Ryker?"

He's back, a smirk of triumph twisting his face as he catches me desperately staring at the screen.

"Your sister says hello. She's enjoying her new school.

She feels happy and safe. I can just only hope it stays that way."

His implied threat turns my blood to ice.

The door pushes open and Junior walks past me with a dismissive air. He laughs at my look of scorn and bounds up the stairs two at a time. I slink to the chair as soon as their car has left the drive, emotionally exhausted. Mia's still kneeling, her eyes downcast. I've been fucking stupid thinking I could toy with her emotions and mine and there would be no backlash.

I want to go to her.

I want to find my sister and run away.

Instead, I sit and stare until she blurs in my vision and do nothing.

# CHAPTER NINE

## RYKER

The banging on the door startles me. There are not many people that know this place exists, even the horse trainers aren't aware of what goes on beneath their stables, so the thought of someone pounding on the door long after everyone has left for the day is unnerving. But a quick glance at the outside camera reassures me. Just the look of the vehicle alone tells me that Cameron, Junior's bodyguard, is the one making the noise. Last time he came here it was to deliver a rack of clothing. I wonder what Junior has in mind for her this time.

I jump up the stairs, taking them two at a time and rip open the door.

"Feeling lonely, big boy?" Cameron pushes past me and thumps down the stairs, pulling out the chair I was sitting on and propping his feet on the other.

"Sure, make yourself at home."

"You've been summoned." Cameron winks and puts his hands behind his head. "Senior wants you to come to dinner at the mansion."

"You're fucking kidding."

"I'm fucking not," Cameron replies. "The old man himself issued the command. I'm here to keep an eye on things while you're away." Cameron's eyes peruse over the screen, a dark smile twisting over his face. "Not a bad gig, if I do say so myself."

"Don't fucking touch her," I say between gritted teeth.

Cameron sucks in air. "So that Marcel guy was right. You do want to taste the goods."

"Fuck up."

"You fuck up."

We both grin as Cameron reaches into his pocket and tosses me the keys to the van. "I've got the family wagon today," he says, referring to the Mercedes parked outside. "Be gentle on her. They're expecting you at the mansion within a couple of hours, so you better get going."

"Any idea why I've been bestowed this honor?"

Cameron shakes his head, closing his eyes as though preparing to go to sleep. "Not a fucking clue. Have fun."

I'm about to walk up the stairs when he calls out again. "What happened to him?"

"To who?"

"That Marcel guy. Something tells me he wouldn't want me here alone with his girls."

"He got let go."

"Oh." Cameron is under no illusion as to what that

means. "Rough," he says. "Were you the one to do it?"

I merely nod and leave, not wanting to think about it.

When Everly and I first arrived at the mansion as kids, we often had dinner with the family. But as time passed and I grew to be more involved in the business, the invitations waned. Everly, of course, still ate with the family on occasion, but I avoided it like the plague. As well as feeling more like a servant at the wrong table, Mrs Atterton had become increasingly interested in me, her hands lingering just a little too long when she touched me, her eyes daring me to do unspeakable things. Katriane Atterton is a stunning woman and I once made the mistake of accepting her advances. It won't happen again. The temptation is there though. Mrs Atterton isn't used to not getting want she wants. None of the Attertons are.

With the van set to cruise control, the trip back to the mansion doesn't take long and soon I am turning down the long driveway, the trees lit up by spotlights. Turning off the driveway before I reach the house, the familiarity of the stables warms me. The second story is dark, no one occupying it in my absence. I jerk the van to a stop and run up the outside stairs, threading my key into the lock. The place smells musty but I've got little time to worry about it. Heading into my bedroom, I open the wardrobe, scanning my clothes for something appropriate to wear for the 'family' dinner.

There's something about the invitation that makes me

wary, makes me think it is just another one of Senior's mind games, but there is no way I can refuse, so I suck it up and pull out a suit. It's usually reserved for my attendance as Mr Atterton's bodyguard at one of his many parties, or one of the auctions, but I haven't got anything else other than jeans and shirts so it will have to do.

Back in the van, I hurriedly make my way over to the mansion and press the doorbell. The butler answers with a blank expression.

"This way," he croons with a swoop of his hand.

"Cheers, Oscar." I smile wickedly and pat the top of his bald head. He pretends to hate it when I do that, but secretly, I think he likes it.

I follow him into the grand entrance, craning my head upward to see the hanging chandelier and sweeping staircase. I usually enter through the back entrance into the kitchen which is humble and pales in comparison to this. Smack damn in the middle of the floor stands Grace. The horse that started it all. Stuffed of course. There's something about it that gives me the creeps. I'm not a fan of dead things pretending as though they are still alive.

"Follow me," Oscar barks, and I grin at him again, invoking an eye roll worthy of the record books.

The mansion is somewhat of an odd building. It's fucking huge, but it hasn't always been that way. It started off as a grand, but modest house and each generation of Attertons have added to it, leaving their mark on both the architecture and the décor. I follow Oscar through the warren of hallways until we reach the dining room. I've never eaten in here before. I've stood to the side and watched as other people sat around the table consuming copious amount of decadent foods, but I've never actually sat at the table. Like the house, it is huge. The placings have been set for five, and briefly, I wonder with a little trepidation who the other person will be. There's something wrong about this whole situation and it's making me uneasy.

Oscar pulls out a chair and I slide into it, trying not to look at the three massive portraits of the Atterton men on the walls. Junior, Senior and the old bastard. Well, not officially, but it's what I like to call them. The old bastard was only alive for a few years when I first got here. They all look strikingly similar, as though the artist has simply changed the outfits to reflect the times. But Senior doesn't look like that anymore. He's spent too much time and money trying to look young that he's ended up making a mess of himself.

While I'm waiting, there's a rumble in the distance, the faint sound of something whacking air. A helicopter. Mr Atterton must have been away, and there's part of me that can't wait to get back to my old life. A life where I'm not responsible for training another human being. But then I think of Mia and the fact that returning to my old life would mean her starting a new one and nausea twists in my gut. Unwantedly, my eyes gravitate to above, where I know the rooms of Senior's girls are. I've been in them often enough to deliver messages, seen each of their rooms decorated in what I assume are Senior's taste for them rather than their own.

For as long as I can remember he's had his collection of girls. The first time I saw them was not long after I came to live with the family. I followed Senior up the stairs, careful to stay concealed from his keen eyes, and hid in the shadows as he keyed in the code and opened a door that had always been locked. The door closed so slowly behind him, I was able to slip in unnoticed. He called out to them the same way as the trainers called to the horses when they were in the paddocks, crooning their names, and holding treats or jewelry in his hands as though they needed tempting. They came out of their rooms, some running into his arms and the others hanging back with fear in their eyes. All of them were beautiful. It makes me sick to think that Junior is starting his own collection with Mia. She must be so scared and confused back in her cell, wondering where I am, wondering why I've deserted her.

The blades of the helicopter slow to a stop once it's landed and not long after, the door opens and the family walks in. But it's not just the family. Everly is there too. I stand, surprised to see her as she runs into my arms and hugs me tightly. Her eyes are wide with excitement.

"He sent the helicopter just to collect me for dinner!" she squeals. "Could you ever imagine such a thing? My classmates were so jealous. It literally landed on the yard in front of the school and they all crowded around wondering who had arrived. I just about died when they said it was here to collect me. Isn't it a wonderful surprise, Ryker?"

She's already untangled herself from me and sat herself down at the table in a poof of pink. I haven't seen the dress she's wearing before and I frown slightly, wondering where she got the money to afford it. But then I catch Senior's eye and I know it was from him. I love and hate his attention to Everly. Love it because it makes her so happy and provides her with all the things I never could. Hate it because he uses it to control me, and I often wonder if there's a darker motive to his attention. Everly's only 16. She's young and innocent of the world the Atterton's live within. I want to keep it that way. I will take her away from this place, as soon as I can figure out how.

Junior slides into the chair next to Everly and smiles thinly. His eyes glance over to her talking animatedly and fall over her body possessively. My hands form fists under the table. Is it not enough that I had to watch him salivate over Mia, do I have to watch him do it over my little sister too?

I grit my teeth together and attempt to smile at Everly as she turns to me, another tale of her classmates spilling from her mouth. She is everything perfect and innocent in the world. I just want her to stay that way.

While Mr Atterton sits at the head of the freakishly oversized table, Katriane sits opposite me, red wine in her hand, sipping on it daintily. She attempts to catch my eye over the rim of the glass and smiles seductively.

"So where have you been, Ryker, hmmm? I've missed seeing your beautiful smile around the house."

Everly slaps the table and laughs. I'm not known for my smile.

"Yeah, where have you been anyway?" she asks just as the first course is laid on the table. My mouth waters at the sight of it. The food back at the stables has been limited.

"Yes," Katrine corrects.

"Yes, what?" Everly asks.

"You said yeah. Yeah is not becoming. Use yes."

"He's actually been working for me," Junior interrupts.

"For you?" Everly lets out a half laugh half snort. "What on earth have you got going on that would need my brother's help? Flipping the pages of your music?" She neatly arranges a mouthful of food on her fork and pops it into her mouth, her eyes darting to Katriane for approval.

"You'd be surprised." Junior winks. "Ryker has proven himself very useful, if not a little over-zealous with my current project. He damn near killed someone who tried to steal something of mine."

"Oh!" Everly's eyes sparkle. "That sounds dangerous, do tell me more."

"It's nothing you need to worry about." My voice is gruff and there's a little hurt in Everly's eyes. Junior's amused gaze snaps to mine and I muster as much warning in my glare as I can.

"So what project are you working on? Composing? Or are you tackling some impossibly hard piece on the piano? I constantly tell my classmates about you. They would die if they heard you play, just die."

"There seems to be a lot of dying going on at your school," Katriane says dryly.

As I lift my wine glass, Katriane's foot brushes against my leg, and I jump, just about spilling the liquid. She looks me directly in the eye as her foot rises higher and higher until it rests on the seat between my legs. I sit up straighter as the heel of her shoe pushes into my crotch. Her face is impassive as she takes another sip of wine.

"So," Senior's loud voice booms, startling me even more. "Tell us more about your school, Everly. Is it everything you wished it to be?"

"Well, yeah, I mean yes." Everly places her cutlery across her plate. "It is everything I imagined it would be and more. The teachers are sensational. I've learned so much since I've been there, it seems so much longer than a few months, but then again, on the other hand, the time has flown by because I've been having so much fun."

"Not too much fun, I hope." Mr Atterton attempts to lift a warning brow but it kind of gets stuck halfway, quivering as though the muscles have forgotten how to respond to the command.

Katriane's foot pushes into me painfully and my dick

unwillingly hardens as she takes another leisurely sip of wine, staring directly at me as though her husband isn't even in the room. I close my eyes and breathe heavily, trying to think of anything other than the pressure of her heel.

"Oh, not bad fun," Everly is quick to reply. "Just good fun. I would never squander the opportunity you've given me by paying for my tuition."

Senior reaches out to pat her hand and it takes all my control not to swipe it away.

"Always such a grateful girl." Senior looks over at me, his eyes boring into my soul. I turn away only to be greeted by Katriane's slow smile. In the end, I drop my gaze to the gold shoe twisting into my lap.

Fuck. This is awkward.

But as Everly prattles on about her new school and everything she's learning, I come to realize the reason Senior invited me to this little soirée.

To remind me of everything I've got to lose.

# CHAPTER TEN

## RYKER

The drive back to the stables seems to take longer than it did before. The road stretches before me as a lonely line of black and my thoughts are just as dark.

Senior was warning me, that much is clear. Maybe he didn't fall for my lies, maybe he knew the torment inside me over ensuring Mia's captivity. I've been stupid to put Everly at risk, but I simply can't resist Mia. I know I can't have her, but it doesn't stop me from wanting her.

She's still sitting under the window, illuminated only by the light of the moon as I stride past the monitors. She doesn't look at me when I walk in. Already, that look of hope, of happiness at my appearance has been tainted. I don't know what else I expected.

I slink down the wall beside her, wanting—no, needing her to look at me.

"Are you okay?"

It's a stupid question, I know. We were lost in our own world, a fantasy world in which we had some sort of choice about our situation. Now reality has come crashing back down, cementing the walls of our world back in place. Senior ensured it.

"I didn't know they were coming." It's a pathetic excuse, but it's the only one I can offer.

She turns to look at me then, those dark eyes searing into my soul. She's so young. So innocent.

"Who is he?"

Closing my eyes, I think of my sister, carefree, full of life and unaware of the monsters around her. Is what I'm doing to protect her worth hurting the only woman I've ever cared about? It's an impossible situation but I know there's no way I could put Everly at risk. Whether she knows it or not, I'm the only person she's got.

It's times like these that I wonder about my parents. Are they still out there? Is my mother mourning the loss of her children, or did she never want us in the first place? But thoughts like those only lead to dark places, and it's dark enough already. I've always been good at blocking them off, but lately it's becoming more and more difficult.

"You're freezing." I grab the blanket off the bed and wrap it over her shoulders. "You'll get sick."

The blanket falls to the ground and her eyes move back to the moon.

"Look at me." I meant it as a question, but it comes out as a command. As if controlled by some other power, she turns to gaze at me and the pain in her eyes causes my heart to constrict.

I should walk out the door and leave her alone.

I should get into the car, grab my sister and leave forever.

I should open the door and let her go free.

But instead, I kiss her, desperate for a reaction, desperate for her to respond in some other way than this coldness.

"Mia, please," I beg, though I don't know what it is I'm begging for.

All I know is this feeling inside me, the one that has ripped open my chest and exposed my heart, beating and pulsing in some empty cavity. Threading my fingers through her hair, I pull her to me, pressing my lips to her passionately, roughly, needing something, anything from her.

"Please," I beg again.

"Please what?" Her voice is flat. "It would be my pleasure to obey your command." She holds my gaze, her eyes somehow a combination of emptiness and defiance.

And then she breaks.

"What do you want from me? If you want me to obey, I can do that. If you want to give me over to him, that's your choice, but I can't do this. I can't do us. I can't be trapped in this imitation of happiness only to have it ripped away from me. I'd rather have nothing than have that. Just tell me what you want."

I want to be free of the Attertons.

I want my sister to be safe. I want her to have everything she ever wished for in life, but most of all I want her to be happy.

But I don't say any of those things, because they are not the words that pound with desperation through my head.

"I want you. I want you free. I want you free to choose me."

Her eyes flash with anger. "But I am not free! He owns me. He owns my body. You're the one who told me that. You're the one who made me chant it over and over until the words got stuck in my head."

Her words push into my mind, forcing flashes of images of the first time I made her come. The way her body trembled, the way her fingers dug into my hair, and the way she cried out. Then I think of the way she scrambled to the corner, fear and confusion showing in her eyes as she tried to hide from me.

Who is this person I've become?

Who is this man that forced himself on her and now demands her love?

Her voice quietens as she pleads with me. "You're the one who holds my freedom in your hands. Just open the door. Let me go."

I turn away, pressing my back against the wall and closing my eyes as her voice cuts me open. It would be that simple. All I would need to do is open the door and set her free. She would walk along the road and in an hour or two, she would find herself back in her hometown. But again, those are not the words I say, because in letting her go, I would be imprisoning my sister. I would be risking my life. And Mia would still never be free.

"It's not that simple. I cannot betray them. They would kill me. They would kill you. They would kill Everly."

I know this to be true because I've seen it. I heard the coldness in Senior's voice when he ordered me to kill Marcel. There was no torment, no emotion at the thought of ending someone's life who had been loyal to him for years. The Attertons may make you think that you mean something to them, but when it comes down to it, they only look after themselves.

"You've already betrayed them by fucking me."

The words sound strange on her lips. Almost blasphemous.

"That's different."

But it wasn't. I know that if Senior or Junior found out what I'd done, my days would be numbered. My only hope would be for them to leave Everly out of it. Punish only me and not her.

And I didn't like to think of what happened between us as fucking. But I guess that's what it was. I thought I was a strong man, but around her, I am weak. Just listening to her utter those words makes my cock hard. I get visions of her stretched on the ground below me.

Calling to me.

Begging for me.

Needing me.

Only me.

But then she puts me through hell, describing things that he might do to her. I try to block her words out of my head, but her voice penetrates my mind and forces the visions on me. My hands are in hers and her fingers dig into the soft flesh of my palm, somehow making her words more real. They force me to think of what Junior might do to her. What he will do to her.

"Enough!" I pull my hands away, pleading with her to understand. If I set her free, my sister is in danger. Mia is in danger. Everyone she cares about is in danger.

But she keeps on pushing, telling me how I'm burned into her skin, how I own her body, torturing me by reminding me of all the things we can never be. "You, Ryker. Only you."

"They know everything about you, Mia. Everything. Do you understand?" I tell her they know about her parents, her best friend, even the little kid next door that she looks after each Friday. "I know what we have between us is twisted. I know we should stop, that no good can come of this, but here, now, us, being with you is the only part of you I will ever have. I can't stop. I don't want to stop. I crave you. I hate that I crave you, but I do. I'll take any part of you I can get." I grip her cheeks between my hands, searching her face for understanding of the situation we are in.

And then I kiss her.

Not a gentle kiss, not a pleading kiss, a kiss of desperation and savagery that stirs reckless desire within.

"I know it is selfish," I say. "I know I shouldn't be doing this, that I'm only hurting you more, but I can't stop."

Locked in each other's gaze, I fight the raging urge to kiss her again. But everything about her is so perfect, so forbidden and so tempting, the floodgates open and I push her to the ground, crawling over her body and kissing her as though I could pour all my emotions into that one action and make her understand.

"Please," she begs, but I don't know whether she is begging for me to stop or begging for me to keep going. It's her actions that answer for her as she tears my clothes off and we become a feverish tangle with our lips locked together as though our kiss could save us from this hell we're in.

And then I push inside her and the world stills.

"You are everything, Mia. Everything." My words are truth and lies. I push deep inside her, wishing I could remove any fraction of distance that separates us.

"We can't keep doing this," her words come out as a whimper, but I ignore them, silencing her with my mouth trailing across her skin, devouring her and committing her to memory.

"It's not safe."

My mouth lingers at her neck, tasting her, inhaling her. "I know. But I want you. I need you."

At my words she cries out, her body rising off the floor to greet mine as a wave of pleasure washes over her. I want to watch her but the clenching of her muscles is too much and I too come undone.

Rolling away, I look up at the ceiling, my heart pounding, my chest heaving with exertion. "Letting you go would be signing your death warrant. I can't do it. I won't do it."

Her hair is in disarray, her body covered in red marks from where I've gripped her skin. "I know." She rolls onto her side, turning to look at me. "What happened to Marcel?"

The image of his body lying in the hole as I shovel dirt on him, eyes unblinking as they stare at me, comes to mind. The red light blinks in the corner. Fuck. I forgot about the camera. Panic blinds me as I get to my feet, the thought of Senior of Junior standing in front of the monitors watching us slicing through my mind like a knife. But it's the middle of the night. There shouldn't be any need to fear. But even still, I've been foolish, putting both Mia and Everly at risk to sate my need.

"You don't have to worry about him hurting you anymore." I lean over to press a kiss to her cheek. "I'll be back in a minute."

I walk out the door, my heart pounding at the thought that we may have been caught but no one is there. The hallway is clear, and I watch the screen as Mia walks into the bathroom, chanting something at her reflection in the mirror. Turning the camera off, I rewind the footage, watching us fuck in reverse until it's back to before I entered the room. And then I press delete and start recording again, all evidence erasing with each second.

She's sitting on the bed when I walk back in, tears rolling down her cheeks without a sound. I kneel between her legs, brushing her tears away.

"Don't cry. I will figure this out. I will keep you safe."

More lies. I want them to be truth. I would do anything for them to be truth, but I'm not even sure I know what that is anymore.

I'm searching her face, looking for any sort of understanding, or maybe it's forgiveness I want when the cold metal of a knife blade presses to my throat. There's almost a peace that descends over me. I'm not surprised. I'm not angered. She could be the one to take my torment away.

"You know I can't just let you leave," I whisper hoarsely. "If you walk out that door, they will find you. They will hunt you down. They will destroy both you and me."

Part of me is begging her to do it. Take that knife and slice it across my throat. I would be done then, no more worry, no more pain. But she would not. My sister would not. I would be leaving them alone in this world.

"Let me go or I'll use this." Her voice wavers and indecision floats in her eyes. I push against the blade until warmth trickles down my neck. I feel as though someone has torn me in two, grabbed two sides of my heart and yanked them apart. Maybe that's why the memory of the stain on the floor is so vivid in my mind. Maybe it's not a memory at all. Maybe it's a premonition.

"I won't do it, Mia. I won't let you die." I swallow, and it exaggerates the feel of the blade against my Adam's apple.

"I'd rather you be with him than die."

Because a world without Mia isn't a world I want to be in. I can't be the one responsible for her death. I can't be the one to let her go.

"This time," she leans close and the scent of her invades me. I close my eyes, taking a deep breath and willing myself the strength to stop her. "You're not the one who gets to decide."

"You won't do it. You can't," I say hoarsely.

"Let me go."

"No." The word rips my throat, causing more pain than the blade.

The heat that sears my shoulder is my first realization of what she's done. I fall to the ground, unable to move, my hands and my legs refusing to work. The edges of my vision start to fill with darkness.

"Mia," I croak.

But she's already gone.

# requestor

# CHAPTER ELEVEN

## REQUESTOR

The taste of her is still on my lips. She's sweet like honey. She coats my mind as a thick glaze, spreading herself through every crevice until I can think of nothing but her. The memory of her voice echoes as I remember the feel of her hand pressed against my hardness, gripping onto it as though she can't wait to be mine, her fingers tightening and stroking, hungry and desperate.

It's all for you, my songbird.

But then my thoughts turn to him. I don't want her there with him for a moment longer. She responded to him too eagerly, too quickly and there was something about the way his expression softened when he looked at her that made me nauseated.

She isn't his.

She is mine.

I jerk the steering wheel, the tires screeching across the tar-sealed road as I turn the car around. I need to see her again. I can't wait any longer for her to be mine. I don't care if Father doesn't think I'm ready. He does not understand the connection between my songbird and me. He is an imbecile, not capable of comprehending the depth of our bond, content with his whores that suck his cock and sate his sexual appetite. He is nothing more than the simpleton I was somehow born to.

The light has faded from the sky and the moon has risen. It's full tonight, as though it is spurring me on, lighting the way to my love. After dinner, after seeing Everly off, I tried to go to sleep but it was pointless. I kept thinking of her. Of my songbird. Needing a distraction, I slipped into my car, wanting to numb my brain with the dim and blurred landscape. I didn't intend on going to see her, but the desire is too strong. Pressing my foot to the floor, the car surges beneath me like a tamed beast.

The desire to see her again pulses through my veins as desperation. I need to see her, to feel her, to taste her. I want those plump lips, lips made for sin to drag across my flesh, bite me, taste me, devour me. I imagine her kneeling before me, eyes cast to the ground, me towering over her in splendor. I would tilt the angle of her chin to gaze up at me and there would be lust in her eyes. Deep-seated lust that would pool in the depths, wanting me, longing for me, craving me. But I wouldn't let her touch me. No. Not the first time. The first time would be all about me and what I wanted. I would do whatever I desired to her body, taking what was rightfully mine.

My thoughts have distracted me from the road and

something flashes out of the corner of my eye. I slow the car, pulling to a stop, curious. Winding down the window, I look out into the night. The light of the moon has drenched the branches of the trees in silver. There's a faint breeze which whispers over the blades of grass making them dance.

But I do not see any movement, any flashes of motion. I wind the window back up, sighing with the knowledge that my brain played tricks on me. It does that from time to time.

Pulling back onto the road, I keep driving until the outline of the stables is visible. The moon rises above the roof, nothing more than a silver circle in the darkness. Slowing to a stop, I cut the engine and listen to the sounds of the night. A bird taking flight. The rustle of leaves in the wind.

I could almost feel peace right now. Almost. If I had my songbird at my side, or locked away in a gilded cage, knowing she was safe, maybe then I would feel it. But right now, staring at the outline of the stable, the hum of my blood starts to increase. I picture Ryker again and the way my songbird's head tilted toward him, subservient and submissive. I rip open the car door and the soles of my shoes crunch on the gravel.

The stairs are difficult to find in the darkness and a wave of anxiety washes over me when I find the door to the rooms below open. The silence inside is deafening. There's a single light bulb illuminating the hallway that makes a buzzing sound, amplifying the hum of my blood.

"Hello?" I call out and my voice strikes me as small and

pathetic in the emptiness. I clear my throat and try again. "Hello? Ryker? Are you here?"

I suppose he is asleep, so I glance around, hoping to see the entrance to his room and demand the code to her door. It infuriates me that I don't already have it. That's when I notice the door to her cell is open.

Striding across the space with urgency, I push the door open, scared what I will find on the other side. Is he in there with her? Is he touching her in ways he shouldn't? There's a small part, just the smallest part that hopes to discover that he is. It would give me the allowance I need to wrap my fingers around his neck, or even press the cold metal of my gun to his temple and pull the trigger. I can almost taste the scent of his blood as it sprays over the walls.

But when my eyes adjust to the darkness of the room, it is not Mia I find. It is Ryker, spread awkwardly on the floor, a pool of blood dampening his clothes.

"Junior?" he croaks.

Even in death, he insists on humiliating me.

"Help." His voice is faint and weak. "I can't move."

I stride over to him, not caring when my shoes leave marks in the blood. "Where is she?"

"She's gone."

"Gone?" I repeat, not comprehending the word. "What do you mean gone?"

"She stabbed me." His breathing quickens. "She escaped."

Rage begins to bubble in my blood, heating it to

excruciating levels. My songbird has flown the coop, set free by the halfwit spread over the floor.

"Call your father." His words are hissed between clenched teeth. The pool of blood that surrounds him spreads further across the floor and I wonder how he survived this long with so little blood left within him.

His death would be no loss to the world. The only person who would mourn him would be Everly. And she would get over it. My father too. He thinks that Ryker is someone worth having around, someone worth saving, but I know better. He's simple and uncouth with not one ounce of passion within him.

To save his life all I would need to do is call my father. Just a quick press of a button and a doctor would be on his way.

But no one knows I came back to the stables. No one knows I am here. All I would need to do for Ryker to leave my life forever would be to walk away.

mia

# CHAPTER TWELVE

## MIA

It feels like I've been running for hours, guided only by the light of the moon. I follow it like a road, hoping it will lead me to safety. My body aches, my thighs are tired and weary, my feet sore and bleeding. And I'm cold. So dangerously cold. Even though I'm covered in a fine sheen of sweat from the physical exertion, the breeze that dances around me freezes it to my skin, turning my blood to ice.

But the beat of my heart is steady, pounding in my chest like a drum, urging me to keep going. I stumble and fall, each time pulling myself back to my feet and forcing myself to keep going.

I don't think of Ryker. I don't picture him lying on the concrete floor, blood seeping from the wound inflicted by the knife stuck in the flesh of his shoulder.

Or, at least, I tell myself I don't. But I have been known to lie.

At first, I think I'm imagining the lights in the distance. They are so faint, just a glimmer of pale yellow, but the closer I get, the more they solidify. They are from the windows of a house. A small farmhouse with a circular driveway and an old truck sitting near the front entrance, the driver's side door flung open as though the occupant has left in a hurry. Crouching low, I hide behind one of the tires, poking my head around to stare through the windows. A shadow passes and my heart beats rapidly, not knowing whether the person inside means safety or danger.

What if it is him?

What if my requestor lives close to the stables and is waiting behind those walls?

The lights illuminating the interior of the house switch off, leaving only the blue hue of the television to see by. I creep closer, hovering under the sill of the window and pop my head up, hoping that no one is watching. There's a sole occupant inside. A man sitting on an over-stuffed chair, beer can in one hand, the other hand stuffed down his pants, eyes glued on the motorbikes racing across the screen. He shifts, moving back into the chair, forcing it to recline and reaches down to flick the handle on the side, releasing the footstool.

I stay, watching him like that until my body screams in protest at the awkwardness of my position. I think back to all I've discovered about my requestor and decide the likelihood that it is him is very slim. But that still doesn't stop the welling nausea in the pit of my stomach as I approach the door. It still doesn't stop the thud of my heart as the volume of the TV gets muted and the man waits for my knock again, uncertain it was what he heard so late at night.

His footsteps echo through the house as he approaches the door. Conflicting emotions pulse through me, my body jerking with indecision. Run or stay? Expose myself for the possibility of safety or stay hidden with the risk of danger. And then suddenly the door is flung open, and the man looms in the frame, his eyes scanning over me curiously.

I open my mouth, but no sound comes out.

"Can I help you?" He crosses his arms over his chest and the movement causes the light behind him to blind me for a moment. "Jesus," he says irreverently. "Are you okay? Are you hurt?"

I try to imagine what he must see as he looks at me. A naked girl covered in bruises with wild hair and fear in her eyes.

"Help me." The words are only squeezed through my throat faintly. I'm leaning against the wall of his house, ready to collapse. The concern in his eyes spells safety, not danger and I long to sink into it. Let go. Slip into a sleep without trepidation.

He sees I'm about to fall and reaches out to grab me, sort of grunting when I fall into his arms. He pulls me inside, scooping his hands under my legs and carrying me over to the couch.

"What happened to you?"

I don't answer. Everything that I've experienced over the last couple of weeks washes over me like waves crashing against rocks. There's a darkness pulling at me, begging for oblivion, for peace.

Something heavy gets draped over me and I feel a little warmer. I pull the blanket close to my chin, hiding my marked flesh from the man standing wide-eyed over me.

"I'm calling the police."

He talks in hushed tones, giving his address, telling them to hurry. And then a small voice floats through the darkness.

"What's happening, Daddy? Who is that girl over there?"

I'm able to blink open my eyes long enough to see the girl watching me from the doorway. She has a pink cotton nightgown on and blonde curls.

"She's just someone who needs our help, darlin'."

Even in my exhaustion, there's something about the affection in his tone that comforts me, in the way he said darlin' that makes the remaining shreds of worry fall away.

I am safe.

I am free.

It overwhelms me and I start to cry violently, not caring as my body convulses with sobs, or as tears and snot run down my face.

"She's cryin', Daddy."

Through my tears, I watch as he scoops the little girl up, much like he did with me earlier, and puts her down on a stool in the kitchen. "She's hurt." He passes the girl the kettle. "We need to help her feel better. Do you think you could make her a cup of tea? I think that would help her feel better, don't you?"

The man keeps glancing over at me, unsure how to respond to my outpouring of grief and relief.

"The police are on their way. You'll be safe soon. They'll get you to a hospital, get you cleaned up." His eyes move down to the blood covering my feet. "You got anyone you want me to call?"

Another wave of uncontrollable crying consumes me, but I manage to croak out the number to my parent's house. He hands me the phone as the ringtone sounds over and over.

*Please pick up.*

They will be in bed.

*Please pick up.*

They will be sleeping.

*Please pick up.*

"Hello?" the voice holds an urgency to it, an expectancy.

The relief that washes over me when I hear her voice is almost painful. "Mum," I manage to sob.

"Mia? Mia, is that you?" Her pitch has risen, choked with tears. "Samuel!" she yells, turning away from the phone. "Samuel, Mia is on the phone! It's Mia! It's Mia!" An excited breath crackles down the line. "Where are you? I'm coming to get you, just tell me where you are."

"I don't know," I wail, and the man takes the phone off me, giving instructions down the phone and letting my mother know he's called the police. Flashing lights reflect across the window.

"Go to the station," he says. "The police have just pulled up. They will meet you there." He listens for a moment as the little girl walks over to me, tea falling over the edges of the cup with each step.

"I'm not sure, sorry. She hasn't said much."

"Here's your cup of tea." She holds the cup out. "I hope it makes you feel better." She leans in closer as her father continues to answer questions from my mother. "Are you scared?" she whispers.

All I can do is nod and pull the blanket closer.

"Don't worry," she says. "My Daddy will look after you." She darts away, her footsteps light on the ground and comes back holding a teddy bear. "Here." She shoves the bear at me. "He always makes me feel better when I'm scared."

Reaching out to take the toy, I pull it close to my chest and cry some more. I cry because I remember being her. I remember being the girl who thought that she was protected, safe, who didn't know the danger that can lurk even in the most placid of places.

And I cry because that girl doesn't exist anymore.

# CHAPTER THIRTEEN

## MIA

Mum clutches my hand tightly, as though if she lets go I might disappear again. The seats we're sitting on are cold and hard. Everything about me is numb.

My skin.

My thoughts.

My memories.

We're at the police station and there's a man who I assume is a detective, although he's not in uniform, looking at me curiously. I can't remember his name. I can't remember anything about him, or even if he's told me his name.

My memories are a blur from the moment the police arrived. Their words were all spoken in hushed tones that jumbled into confusion inside my head. They asked what happened, where I had been, who had hurt me. So many questions. Enough to make my head hurt.

I wish I could say I answered them confidently, but I'm not even sure if I answered at all. It was like I was caught in a dream, just a spectator of all the commotion going on around me. A policewoman sat beside me in the back seat of the car and rested her hand on my thigh. I remember it feeling heavy and hot, burning my skin. Everything inside me wanted to wrench it off, but it was like I was frozen, unable to do anything but watch.

I felt nothing until I saw my mother and then I felt her tears soaking into my shoulder. My father's strong arms wrapped around me too and I heard his voice, deep and comforting, but I couldn't comprehend what he was saying. Things jumbled in a jerking fast-forward motion until I found myself here, sitting on the hard chair and staring into the eyes of someone who is frustrated with my lack of answers, though he's doing his best not to show it.

A heavy blanket is wrapped over my shoulders, the one from the farmhouse that the man insisted I keep when the police came to collect me. I keep glancing down at it as though it holds the answers to the questions I can't fathom.

"What about where you were held? What can you tell us about it? Anything would be helpful, anything at all."

A pen is poised on top of paper, waiting.

"Stables." My voice is far away as though it is coming from someone else and I am only a spectator to the answer.

"Stables?" the man repeats.

I close my eyes and see the white breath of the horses escaping into the night. "There were horses."

"And you were kept in one of these stables? Is that where

they kept you?"

I shake my head. "Below."

The pen is put back on the desk. "Below?"

"Below the stables, down the stairs."

"And where are these stables? How far away? How long were you running before you got to the farmhouse?"

Tears gather and fall. "I don't know. It could have been hours, it could have been minutes."

The door opens, and a different man walks in, making me jump in fear. My mum squeezes my hand harder and smooths my hair. The man looks over me and my skin crawls as I wonder if he could be him. Could this man with the cold eyes and pocked skin be my requestor? There's a folder in his hands. His fingers are long and pale, reminding me of Marcel.

"Here's the statement from the farmer." He places the folder on the desk. "Nothing all that helpful."

The man behind the desk's response is clipped. "That will be all, thank you." He dismisses the man and he leaves with barely a glance my way. Not my requestor, after all. I don't think.

"And the name of the men that held you, do you remember them? Did they call each other anything? Get you to call them something?"

I swallow the lump in my throat. His eyes dart to my mother.

"Perhaps it would be best if we spoke to Mia alone."

"No!" I shake my head violently, tears springing to my eyes once more. "No," I say again, but this time gentler.

Mum pats my knee, strokes my hair, and smooths the blankets, a constant flow of motion.

"I'm not going anywhere," she whispers. "Do you remember anything? Anything at all?"

"Marcel." The name rips from my throat and I squeeze my eyes tightly, willing away the memory of him that comes flooding through my mind.

"Marcel?" The man repeats, just like he's repeated each of my answers, though whether it is to clarify or challenge, I'm unsure.

"Do we have to do this now?" my father says, frustrated. He leans against the wall, arms crossed over his chest, and glares at the man asking the questions. "Can't it wait until tomorrow? Until she's had some sleep, some food in her stomach? Hasn't she been through enough?"

I want to cry at the pain in his voice. Instead, I lift my head and manage a wobbly smile. Tears well in my father's eyes and he clears his throat as if it will dislodge them.

"It's okay, Dad. I need to do this."

Forcing myself to picture him, I describe Marcel in detail. The blackness of his curly hair. The sinister way he smiled. I tell them everything he said to me about the man who requested me and how it is the family business. My mother covers her mouth when I speak of some of the more explicit details, but I don't spare her. I can't. It's like I've opened a floodgate and the flow of information is unstoppable. I explain every aspect of my life in the cell in detail, right down to the red stone in the floor and the scent of the shampoo in the shower.

But when it comes to talking about Ryker, his name gets stuck in my throat.

"And this Marcel," the detective prompts, "he was the one who was…" he pauses his eyes flicking between my parents before coming to rest on me again. "He was the one training you?"

I shake my head, but I can't bring myself to look at him.

"There was someone else? The man you said requested you?"

I shake my head again, twisting my fingers together as they lay in my lap. "Marcel was a trainer but not mine," I whisper. "And the man who requested me only came to visit the once, but I was blindfolded, and I couldn't hear all that well, so I don't know much about him other than what he said."

"And what did he say?"

The pen rises off the desk again, poised between the detective's fingers.

"He called me his sweet songbird."

"His songbird?" His insistence on repeating my answers grates.

"Yes, and he said he couldn't wait until I was his."

The policeman has to lean forward to hear my answers, my voice is so quiet.

"Do you sing?"

"She's got a beautiful voice, so beautiful," my mother answers for me.

I cringe, not knowing if I will ever be able to sing again. If I'll ever be able to return to the thing I love, knowing it was what attracted him to me.

"So it would make sense to conclude he had heard you sing before."

The pen starts to scrawl across the page. "I'll need a list of everywhere that you've sung in public over the past year. But," he looks up at me, "you still haven't told me the name of the man who trained you. Do you remember it? Did you ever hear it?"

I blink back tears ignoring the knot of pain at the base of my throat. "I don't even know if it's his real name."

"It's probably not." The detective attempts a small smile. "But it still might help."

Closing my eyes, I'm taken back to my cell, to Ryker's eyes, so tormented, so conflicted.

In the background, the detective talks to my parents. "She could be feeling some sort of emotional bond to…" I block the sound of his voice out, not wanting to hear the words he's about to say. The words which I've thought all too often myself.

"Ryker," I say, interrupting him. "His name was Ryker."

The pen scribbles across the paper, the noise invading my head and burning across my brain.

"Ryker?"

I grit my teeth together and Mum squeezes my hand as though she is trying to send me strength through the connection.

The detective's deep voice is murmuring again though I've blocked myself from the words. I think back to Ryker tearing the clothes from my body as I swung from the chains. I try to remember the bite of the metal, the terror that had settled within me. Those are the things I need to remember. Not the way I felt when he looked into my eyes. Not the feel of his mouth on mine. Not the roughness of his hands as he ran them over my flesh.

"We will take you down to the hospital soon. We'll need to get a rape kit done," The detective is saying when I tune back into the conversation.

"I wasn't raped. Not really. Not in the way you're thinking."

Dad clenches his fists. Mum's hand on my hair freezes mid-stroke. The detective lifts a single brow.

"Marcel," I swallow, "he…" My father walks out the door, his jaw set in a hard line, tears in his eyes. "He put his…" words fail me and I drop my eyes to the ground, wishing I had a red stone to fix my gaze on.

The detective clears his throat. "Mia," he says softly, more softly than he's spoken before, "would you prefer to talk to a female officer? There's none on duty at the moment but we could call Officer Hardy down from the city. She would be more than hap—"

"It's fine," I bite out, my eyes darting to the window where my father paces the hallway, hands threaded through his hair as though he's tugging on the ends. "I'm fine. I just need a minute or two."

The detective gets up from his desk. "I'll go get us some water."

As soon as he's out the door, I turn to my mother, hoping she will understand. Needing her to understand. It's so hard to say the words aloud.

"I don't want you to think… I don't want you to—" Tears start to fall again, the intensity cutting off my words.

My mother clasps my cheeks between her hands. Her gaze flicks between my eyes, boring into me. "There is nothing you can say that will change the way I feel about you. Do you hear me, Mia Cooper? Nothing that those men did or didn't do can change a thing. And there's nothing you can tell me that you did or didn't do that will change the fact that I love you. I love you, baby girl. I always have and I always will. If you need me to leave while talking to the policeman, I can do that, but never, even for a moment think that anything you say will make me think differently of you Mia. Nothing. None of this is your fault." She pulls me close and strokes my hair. "I love you. Nothing will change that. Nothing can change that. I know this is hard. You've finally got free, finally home and now you're having to relive it all over again."

She just holds me as I cry. She doesn't know the truth. She doesn't know I willingly fell into my captor's arms. I'm overwhelmed, tired by the questioning, the mental exhaustion of reliving my escape and my captivity over and over.

"I just want to go home," I manage to sob.

Mum smooths my hair again and pulls back to look me in the eye. "No more questions," she promises. "But they will need to gather any evidence they can before you go home. Do you think you can do that?"

I nod numbly, knowing I have no other choice. If I want the police to have a shot at capturing my requestor they will need all the evidence they can.

The policeman walks back in and sets a jug of water and some plastic cups on his desk. After sitting down, he clears his throat and opens his mouth to speak, but my mother talks before he can.

"That's enough questions." Her tone leaves little room for argument. "We will go to the hospital, but then we are going home. My girl needs to go home. She needs a good night's sleep in her own bed."

"According to Mia herself, the person who requested her knows everything. They know who you are and where you live. It would be best if you and your daughter—"

"I don't care what you think is best. I know what is best. I will be taking Mia home. I will stay with her and never leave her alone. Post a guard outside the door. Have someone watching the house at all times. I don't care what you do, but you will do everything you can to ensure her safety at home."

"Mrs Cooper." The policeman places the pen back down. "I really think that you and—"

My mother leans forward, the expression on her face fierce. "I don't care what you think." She blinks once. "This is what is going to happen."

# CHAPTER FOURTEEN

## MIA

Each time I fall asleep, my body jerks back awake, startling me with terror prickling over my skin. But then I feel the hand of my mother resting on my shoulder, I see the crack of light coming through from the hallway, the familiar color of my walls, the smell of my bedding, and I know I am safe. For now, anyway. I can't help but think of my requestor out there, watching and waiting for the perfect time to take me again.

I've done my best to block out going down to the hospital. The way they examined my body, checking it for each and every injury, reminding me of the early days in the cell and the way Ryker would run his hands over me, getting me used to his touch, teaching me not to flinch. Being with the nurse was just the same. I went into some trance-like state, only focusing on the voice and smile of my mother instead of what the nurse was doing and why she did it. I blocked my mind off to the scraping under my fingernails and the combing through my hair.

When it was done, my father drove us home, a police car following our every move, me in the back seat, my head pressed against the window and looking at the sky.

Once home, I hopped under the stream of hot water and let it burn until my skin turned red. Getting into my familiar pajamas, I lifted the covers and climbed into bed, my mother lying down beside me, but my nightmares mean I can't get to sleep.

Beside me, my mother breathes easily. Lifting her hand, I slide out from the bed and walk over to the window, tugging the curtains open and sinking to the floor with my back against the wall. I hug my knees close to my chest, my chin resting on the bent caps, and stare out at the night sky. Searching the stars, I look for the ones shaped in the pattern of a cross, hoping that somehow, if I find them, they will tell me if Ryker's okay. But they aren't out tonight, hidden by cloud. Or I can't find them. I can only see my own reflection.

I think back to standing in front of the small mirror in the bathroom of my cell and chanting the words that gave me the strength to escape. "You were a captive. He hurt you, broke you. You do not love him." But the girl in the window looks back at me with only one word on her lips.

Liar.

I must have fallen asleep there with my back pressed to the wall because I wake to the scent of freshly baked bread.

Pulling myself from the warmth of the blankets, I drape my dressing gown over my shoulders and head for the bathroom. Turning the water to scolding, I watch as steam fogs up the mirror.

"You do not love him," I whisper to the girl looking back at me. Her skin has a little more color to it. Her eyes a little brighter. Her flesh isn't so bruised with abuse. But I still don't recognize her. She's a stranger, this girl who stares back at me.

A stranger who longs for the man who held her captive. It suddenly dawns on me that I will never see him again. He will never take me in his arms. I will never see his forehead deepen with frown lines. I will never look into those ocean-blue eyes. An empty void threatens to overwhelm me. I feel both pain for the loss of him and guilt for that pain.

It's only when the fog completely blurs my vision that I step into the shower. I don't flinch at its heat. I welcome the burn. The pain. Because that's what I cling to. Pain is the only thing that makes sense at the moment. The only thing I can relate to.

I stay under the heat of the water until it turns cold, and then I step out, eyeing the clothing I had placed on the floor and wonder if I will ever be the same girl again.

If I even want to be the same girl.

Every part of me longs to return to that time of before, but if I did, I would have to let go of the memory of him. My emotions are in constant battle.

The relief of freedom.

The worry of capture.

The guilt of regret.

Before I walk into the kitchen, I plaster on a smile of before. The girl before she was taken. The one who laughed and smiled and told jokes. Not the stranger left in her place. But my smile feels wrong, foreign, as though it's meant for someone else now and not for me.

"Mia!" Roxy flies into my arms before I could even register she was sitting at the table and hugs me fiercely. "I was so worried about you." She squeezes the air out of my lungs. "Why didn't you call? I would have come over straight away. I would have—"

My mother gently peels Roxy's arms off me. "She's been here since first thing. I told her you were still sleeping but she wouldn't leave."

"Liar." Roxy pokes her tongue out at my mother. "I've only just arrived. I was in the city visiting the Fam. I missed you!" Roxy hugs me again and I laugh. It's a genuine laugh too. With Roxy, there's no exaggerated gentleness, no allowance for what I might have been through. She treats me exactly as she would have before and it does me good.

"I've missed you too." I squeeze her back. She feels so small in my arms, reminding me of Star. I wonder what's happened to her, if she's still trapped below the stable or if they've moved her with the fear of getting caught.

"Why don't you two go talk in the other room while I

make some breakfast. Dad's down at the bakery, but I'll whip something delicious up."

Roxy hooks her arm through mine and drags me through the doorway and into the lounge. "I suppose you'll be hungry. Did they, you know," she narrows her eyes, looking over my body, "feed you and stuff? My god, Mia, this is so strange. I don't really know what to say. Are you okay? Did they, um, did they—"

We flop down onto the couch.

"Let's just not talk about it, okay? Let's talk about something else. Anything else. I just need to feel normal again."

She flashes a smile. "Gotcha. Right. Mindless chatter. I'm usually good at mindless chatter so, um, let's think." She starts to prattle on and I relax back into the couch, feeling more like myself than I have in weeks. She's always been the chatter to my silence. Her voice is soothing, giving me a little hope that life could return to the way it was before. But as she talks, something catches my eye out the window. There's a car parked across the street. It's a fancy car, one of the sleek modern ones with tinted windows and shiny rims. But through the tint of the window, I can make out the silhouette of a figure watching the house. I sit up, straining for a better look while not exposing myself to the window.

"Mia? Mia?" Roxy's touch on my leg makes me jump. "Mia are you okay? What are you staring at?"

"Nothing." I dismiss my fears. There's a policeman

stationed outside. Surely if there was anything to worry about, they would have it sorted.

"Are you sure? You look as pale as a ghost."

I laugh. But this time it's strained and Roxy just frowns, knowing I'm lying.

"I'm just a little on edge," I say to her.

"Well, duh. You've kind of just got home from being kidnapped." She laughs, but then her face falls and she reaches out to rest her hand on my knee. The moment makes me freeze and the hot and heavy feeling I had in the back of the police car strikes me again, cutting off my air. I get to my feet and start pacing around the room, trying not to look at the car still parked over the road and failing.

Roxy stands and walks over to the window. "Oh," she exclaims when she sees what I'm staring at. "I didn't think. I should have said something. It's my car. Dad bought me a new one because he went all safety conscious and stuff because," she flashes a smile, "well, just because."

I know I should feel relief, but I don't. "Who is the person inside?" I almost whisper the words, a panicked feeling creeping up inside me.

She places a hand on my arm. "It's just Remy. He really wanted to come and see you. He's been so worried, but I told him he wasn't allowed to come inside until I made sure that you were," she screws up her nose, "you were okay and shit."

I laugh at her bluntness, relief washing over me when I

realize I had let my paranoia get the better of me. "He can come in."

"Are you sure? He's fine waiting in the car. He knows that—" She shrugs, choosing not to finish her sentence.

After assuring her that I'm fine with her brother coming inside, Roxy goes out to him. Remy embraces me awkwardly, holding me just a little longer than necessary. Even though they are twins, they aren't identical, so it surprises me each time I see them together of how similar they look. Not because of their natural physical features, but because they have the same spiked hair and the same strange sense of style.

Mum calls out, letting me know that breakfast is ready and we all pile into the kitchen after she swears she made enough for all of us. Remy sits in the chair next to mine and he's so close, I can feel the heat of his body. It takes all my willpower not to shift my chair away and place distance between us. I know I have nothing to fear from him but there is always a question prickling in the back of my mind.

What if?

But I push it aside. Last night, I gave the police what details I could of the man from the bar and the one from the coffee shop. I even told them about the man at the pool, though I seriously doubted if he could be my requestor. There was too much of a simplicity to him.

For a moment, as I look around the table at the familiar faces before me, I feel at peace. Probably the most peace I've felt since escaping. It gives me the smallest of hopes that maybe, just maybe, one day I will be able to sit here with my time in captivity being nothing more than a horrid part of my past.

# CHAPTER FIFTEEN

## MIA

"Let's start with the one you said was called Ryker." The sketch artist sits before me, partially hidden by the screen of a computer, a sketchpad resting on her lap. "Is there anything in particular that stood out about him? Just tell me the first thing that pops into your mind."

His eyes.

"I'm not sure," I stutter.

After Roxy and Remy left, Mum drove me back down to the police station to complete my interview. Once the detective had finished talking to me, he led me into the room with the sketch artist, hoping my memory would dish up the physical attributes of the men who had kept me captive. Part of me wanted to tell him that he was concentrating on the wrong people, that it was my requestor and not Ryker that they needed to be looking for, but I know any information about Ryker and Marcel could lead them to my requestor. Even still, it feels like an act of betrayal to describe him to the woman before me.

"Let's start with the eyes," she says, as though she had read my mind. "What color were they?"

I close my eyes as though struggling to remember when in reality they are still vivid in my mind. The way they turned down at the corners giving him the faintest hint of melancholy. The way they were hooded and heavy and scorched with lust when they looked at me.

"Blue. I think they were blue."

They were blue and green and gray. They were the color of the ocean during a storm.

"And what about the shape? Were they rounded? Almond shaped? Were there wrinkles in the corners? Could you see the whites above his irises or did his eyelids hang heavy?"

I start shaking my head before she finishes talking. "I'm not sure."

"It's okay," she assures me, pulling some pieces of paper off the desk and handing them to me. "Have a look over these. See if anything looks familiar, reminds you of him."

I stare at the hand-sketched eyes in varying shapes. None of them look like Ryker's. None of them portray the torment and the conflict that dance within them, but I point to ones marked almond shaped and hand back the paper with a shrug. She scratches on the paper, drawing goodness knows what as I have hardly given her any details.

"What about his nose?" she asks next.

Again, I shrug. "It was just a nose," I whisper and wonder if she knows that I'm lying.

Using both hers and mine as a frame of reference, she asks how wide it was, how straight, how elongated, if the end turned upwards or downwards.

I'm silent the whole time she sketches, my eyes skipping around the near-empty room and trying not to look at what she is drawing in case, if by some miracle, it really does resemble Ryker.

She flicks her gaze back over to me. "His lips?"

Full and soft and pink with the bottom lip drooping slightly.

"I don't know what you want me to say." My voice breaks a little when she narrows her eyes. "He had a beard."

Sighing softly, the woman opens one of the desk drawers and pulls out a folder. "Have a flick through here and see if anyone seems familiar." She gets to her feet. "I'll be back soon." And then she's gone, leaving me alone in the room. A room which is small and has a single window that lets in a patch of light that falls over the desk.

Drawing in a shaky breath, I start to flick through the pages of mug shots, scared I'll find Ryker looking back at me. But I don't. None of the faces are familiar, all of them are too rough, too thuggish to be the man I fell for. But just as I hear the clipped steps of the sketch artist coming back along the hallway, one face leaps out at me. He's younger, years and years younger, but I'm certain it's him. He looks so innocent and almost sweet. The sketch artist walks past me and takes her seat on the other side of the desk.

"Here," I say, handing the folder back. "That man is Marcel."

She snatches the folder, pulling it close. "Are you sure?"

The urge to roll my eyes is real. It seems no matter what I say, someone has to repeat it as though I'm uncertain of my own mind. But then I remember all of the vague answers, the hesitant details and think that maybe I'd do the same in their situation.

The look on the woman's face shows a little surprise and I wonder if there's the possibility the police don't believe me. They've checked every stable, and every empty building within a 50km radius and assured me that there were no hidden cells beneath them. In fact, this photo of Marcel is the first solid piece of evidence I've given them.

"Do you want to stop in for a coffee?" Mum glances over at me as her hands rest on the steering wheel.

We've just been down at the police station. Again. The photo of Marcel proved unfruitful, his family claiming to have not seen him in years, and all the tests came back from the lab as inconclusive. Although the police are still trying, there's a wariness in the detective's tone that wasn't there before. Wariness and skepticism.

They've talked to the man at the pool, they've talked to the man who tried to buy me coffee, but both of them have alibis. It's only the mystery man from the bar that they haven't been able to find, and I think they are beginning to doubt he even exists.

Mum taps my knee. "Coffee?"

She slows down as we pass the café, waiting for my answer. I look at all the people inside, some lining up to place their orders and others already sitting at the table, sipping on the bitter liquid and shake my head. Even though I've been home for days, I'm just not ready yet. I keep jumping when people talk too loudly or coming out in a sweat if they sit too closely.

"You sure?"

I let out a frustrated sigh of air and Mum looks over at me apologetically. "I'm sorry," she says. "I just think it would do you some good, you know. Get out and about a little. Discover that the world isn't all bad."

I blink away tears and stare out the window at the passing shops and stores. Our town is a little town. One that I used to feel safe in. But now, with every new face, I wonder if it's him. With every lurking shadow, my heart starts pounding faster. My ears strain to hear strange voices, trying to place them as the man who called me his songbird. But if he's still out there, he's just waiting.

To anyone looking on from the outside, there is nothing wrong with me. My scars are invisible. My bruises are faded and hidden. It's hard for them to know the torment that's in constant battle in my mind. The fear that he will try to take me again. The slight desire that he would so I would know if Ryker's okay.

The police assured me that the likelihood of my requestor trying to take me now is slim. The officers stationed outside our house have gone, although they still drive past regularly, just to pacify my mum.

Life should be returning to normal.

But it's not.

Ryker is constantly on my mind. I dream of him. Think of him. I replay every conversation, every interaction in my head, but instead of the terror I felt during some of those moments, it has been replaced with longing.

Yesterday was the first day Mum went back to work. And I got my period. Even though relief flooded me that I wasn't pregnant, there was also a sadness I didn't quite understand. It was like the final connection to Ryker was severed. As soon as my mother left the house, I phoned every hospital I could think of asking if anyone had been brought in with a stab wound to the shoulder. Of course, it was pointless. I was only met with clipped replies that they couldn't give out that sort of information and annoyance that I had wasted their time by asking in the first place.

That night, I lay in bed and told myself I never loved him. The only reason I felt any attraction toward him at all was because of the situation. He showed a little kindness when I needed it. But in reality, I had only known him within the confines of the walls of a cell. Who he was outside those walls was unknown to me. Everything he told me could have been a lie. Was probably a lie.

But then I think of him sinking to his knees, and the way he looked at me and I ache for him. He invades my mind by day and my dreams by night. I constantly remind myself of who he is, what he did, but my heart won't be told. It longs for him. Aches for his touch with painful precision.

But I will keep telling myself I don't love him until it's no longer a lie.

As if my brain enjoys toying with me, I catch a glimpse of a man out the window. He's walking down the street, and I can only see him from behind, but there's something about the way he's walking, something controlled in his stance that reminds me of Ryker.

Immediately, my heart leaps into my throat. "Stop the car."

Mum looks at me quizzically.

"Stop the car!" I say more urgently.

She slows down and pulls to the side of the road. I open the door before the car comes to a complete stop and climb out, starting to run down the road after the man who looks so much like Ryker.

With each step, I tell myself it's not him. But with each step my heart pounds even more, convincing my body that what my brain is telling it is a lie.

The man has on a cap, his head bent down toward the ground. His shoulders are hunched slightly, something I've never seen in Ryker before but maybe his injury has affected the way he moves. It would make sense.

When I get close to him, I freeze, unsure what to do. Part of me knows that if I see his face, my heart will sink because it won't be him. But still part of me hopes.

"Ryker?" I almost whisper his name.

The man keeps walking, but that's when I notice the headphones covering his ears. Taking a deep breath, I reach out and tap him on the shoulder.

The man looks behind him with a curious glance, and just as I expected, my heart sinks.

It's not him.

"Why hello there." The man smiles brilliantly and tugs his headphones from his ears. "Is there something I can help you with?"

"I'm sorry, I thought you were someone else."

The man's eyes travel over me and he lifts a brow appreciatively. "I can be anyone you want, if you'll let me." He winks.

Before, with an encounter like this, I would roll my eyes and walk away, but now, bile rises in my throat. I turn away from the man, trying to hide my shaking hands, but as I do, he reaches out and grabs my backside, digging his fingers into the flesh and whistling low and long. Rage ignites, and I whirl around and slap him, leaving him reeling back in surprise.

"Bitch!" he hisses, holding a hand to his cheek. "I was just being friendly."

"Friendly?" my mother says, marching up to the man,

hands on her hips. She stands so close to him the man has to take a couple of steps back and almost stumbles.

My rage subsides as quickly as it rose, and I actually chuckle. Next to this man, my mum is small. Small but savage.

"What about grabbing my daughter's bottom without permission is friendly?" There is fire in my mother's eyes.

"You're crazy, lady." The man tries to back away, but there's a parked car behind him and he just ends up pressed against the side, wedged between it and my mother.

"Answer me!" my mother demands. "Tell me what is friendly about it?"

"I—I—" The man looks around as though he can't quite comprehend what is happening. "It was just a bit of fun."

"Fun?" My mother smiles coldly. "Well then, I shall have a little fun of my own." Without hesitation, she reaches out and grabs the man's crotch viciously. He howls and bends over in pain as my mother walks away, rubbing her hands together as though washing them of his filth.

I just stand, wide-eyed and stare at her.

"Come on. Let's get you home."

I follow her to the car wordlessly and climb into the passenger's seat.

"Sorry about that." Mum buckles herself in. "But I just saw red when he touched you like that. I should have had better control."

"Better control?" I laugh. "That was awesome."

"Awesome or not, I shouldn't have let my anger get the better of me." She shifts the stick into gear and pulls out onto the street. "What made you chase after him, anyway?"

I look out the window as we pass the man walking awkwardly down the road. "I thought he was someone I knew."

"Who?" Mum doesn't look at me, but I know she's curious.

I stare at my hands on my lap.

"One of them? One of the men who took you?"

I nod, keeping my eyes down. Tears are threatening again, and I don't want her to see them.

"But why would you chase after him? Why wouldn't we just go to the police?"

I don't want to tell her the truth. I don't want to tell her it's because every day I hope to see Ryker, that I miss him, that despite everything he helped do to me, I still want him.

"I didn't know it was him for sure. Turns out I was right."

She knows I'm not telling the truth, but she doesn't push me.

"How about we invite Roxy over for a movie night? Watch something light-hearted and funny like we used to. Would you like that? Get things back to normal?"

I smile and nod.

Normal.

I don't even know what that is anymore.

# requestor

# CHAPTER SIXTEEN

## REQUESTOR

I lift the strip of material to my nose and inhale deeply. It smells of her. Of sweetness and innocence that I long to ruin.

I wanted to take her back straight away, but my father forbade it. He said it would be too dangerous with the police watching her so intently, with her mother never leaving her side and her father stalking the neighborhood at night like some deranged vigilante. At first, it enraged me. She was mine. She belongs in my arms, trapped in my cage and no one else's. I had visions of what I could do to my father, all the ways I could inflict punishment upon him for keeping me away from what is mine. I had to lessen my seething rage with music, pounding at the keys of the piano, and plucking the strings of a cello until my fingers bled. For hours I had locked myself away, too scared of what I would do if I allowed myself freedom. Thoughts and visions of her were too strong.

But the risk was too big.

My songbird would be mine.

I just needed to be patient. A useless virtue, but one I needed to exercise in order for my plan to succeed. I would wait, like my father instructed, but I wouldn't wait forever.

So I content myself with watching her from afar. It becomes somewhat of a game, lurking in the shadows as she sits, staring at the stars out her window, unable to sleep, thinking of me. Following her to the police station and resisting the urge to snatch her away while she sits in the car as her mother speaks to the detective, a man who personally knows how deep the pockets of my family truly are.

It is an exercise in control. A way for me to demonstrate to my father that I'm no longer the child he thinks I am.

My father is worried. He doesn't want his perfect reputation to be tainted by Ryker's mistake, but I know that the police will never trace her back to me. How could they? Not even she knows who I am and there is no fear of anyone else talking. They are either too loyal or buried in the dirt.

I have begun to take pleasure from my sinister role as her stalker. It is a thrill to be the eyes burning in the dark. I know she can sense me, feel me. Feel the intensity of my need for her, even from afar.

She is becoming bolder, venturing out of her cocoon of safety. Even now, as she sits on the couch, her eyes glued to the book in her lap, I can sense a peace to her smile. Her fear has begun to subside. She's beginning to relax into her old life, making the thought of ripping her away again that much more pleasurable.

With me, her life will be controlled. She will live only to satisfy me, please me. I will take the talent she has no idea is within her and bring it to the fore, bend it to my will until she is beyond perfection.

My cock hardens just at the thought.

I can picture her now, her hands tied behind her back, her face upturned, tears welling in her eyes and her lips trembling. She will open on my command and I will feed myself into her. She will suck on me hungrily, desperately, increasing my hardness as I push deeper into her throat. I will cup the back of her head with my hand and force her onto me until she gags to be set free, her body convulsing as it screams for air. But I won't give it to her. I will keep her there, stuffed against me and reach down to dig my fingers into the plump flesh of her ass. She will try to get away. I know she will try to get away but there will be nowhere for her to go because she will be trapped in a gilded cage of my making, existing only for me. She will fear me, but she will love me. She will beg for me to do bad things to her.

And I will break her.

Despite the coldness to the night, my blood is on fire just thinking about her. My cock is rock hard but as demented as I know I can sometimes be, I'm not going to be caught jerking off while watching her in the darkness.

I have a plan, but I must be patient in allowing her to think that she is safe. It will make our time together that much more potent. The thought of it makes my father's denial of taking her almost bearable.

But in the meantime, I need to get laid. I need a cunt to sate my straining cock. Flicking through the contacts of my phone, I dial a number, clearing my throat of its husky desperation.

"You home?" I ask as soon as she answers, returning to my car and starting the drive to her house.

"You're in town?"

The hitch to her voice tells me she wants me. She always wants me. The slut is nothing like my songbird. She is simply a way to relieve an itch and a damn sight cheaper than a hooker. She's the disguise I've worn for months. And since she comes from a wealthy family, being seen with her in public comes with the approval of my parents.

When she opens the door, she's dressed only in a translucent nightgown. The swell of her huge breasts is visible through the material, her nipples peaking merely at my appearance. I know she's wet for me. She's always wet for me. It's why I keep her around.

She looks at me with a 'come-fuck-me' gaze as I step across the threshold, wrapping my fingers around her neck and pushing her to the wall. Her eyes roll back in her head. She likes it rough. It's not as arousing as if she didn't, but at least she can satisfy my desire without causing any problems. She's a mask. A cover to hide my darker desires.

I take her lips, plundering her mouth with my tongue.

Even with my hands wrapped around her neck, she's desperate for me. I bet her wetness is leaking down her legs at the thought of what I'm going to do to her.

I've always been rough with her. She's never wanted anything else. So I tear at her gown, ripping it until her breasts are exposed. She gasps for air as I loosen my grip and slap her bouncing tits. Her nipples harden even more, and I take one between my fingers, twisting and pulling, pinching and tugging until she rises on her tiptoes, begging for me to stop but not meaning a word of it. Then I lower my head and bite. A wave of lust jolts through me when she gasps once again.

"On your knees," I command, remembering the fantasy of my songbird. She falls to the ground and starts to pull my cock from its confines. She's eager. Too eager and it ruins the illusion. Her face isn't wet with tears, and instead of a trembling mouth, she licks her lips in anticipation.

I push her away and she falls to the ground, looking up at me with curiosity. "Did I do something wrong?"

I slap her across the face. "Turn around. On all fours."

She scrambles to obey like the good little bitch that she is, and I spread the cheeks of her ass wide. She glistens for me, her moisture so thick it's smeared over the inside of her thighs.

I plunge into her roughly, but she can't take the force, her chest hitting the ground, so I steady her hips with my hands as I fuck her relentlessly. She moans. She groans. She

166

whimpers and pleads, and it messes with my fantasy. Reaching down I yank her hair, jerking her head back, her throat tight.

"Shut up."

But my words only make her groan louder.

Her hair is spiked between my fingers and I tug roughly, rough enough that a squeal emits from her mouth. Taking her from this angle means if I squint enough I can pretend she is my songbird. But she keeps moaning and pleading, telling me to fuck her harder, make her hurt.

"Fuck. Up." I punctuate the words with thrusts.

This is physical, nothing else. There is no spiritual connection between us. No coming together of souls. It pales in comparison to what my songbird and I will experience, but it's enough for me to empty my seed. Enough for me to dull my lust.

I withdraw from her and she rolls over, her tits heaving with each labored breath. She's enraptured with me. She thinks what we have is special.

Pathetic whore.

I treat her as nothing more than a fuck-toy and she laps it up.

She blinks at me through a haze of lust. "When will I see you again?"

"I'll call you," I say, stuffing my cock back into my pants and doing up the zipper.

She bites her bottom lip as though I would find it

appealing.

"Make sure you do."

I leave her with torn clothes and my spunk dripping from her as I walk out the door.

She's nothing more than a way to pass the time until my songbird is mine.

mia

# CHAPTER SEVENTEEN

## MIA

Roxy looks at me seriously as we sit in the window of the coffee shop. Around us, the world continues as though it isn't broken. As though it is the same world as before. People smile and laugh. They shop and talk. Some walk quickly, and others stroll past the window without any sense of urgency.

"I think you need to face your fear." Roxy picks up the marshmallows on the edge of her saucer and plops them into her drink.

"Excuse me?" I take a sip of the hot liquid. The scent takes me back to the cell with Ryker, of how good caffeine tasted after weeks of missing it. "Exactly which fear are you referring to? I am not holding a spider."

Roxy rolls her eyes. She's been my constant companion since my return and has been steadily drawing me out of my self-inflicted shell.

"Singing? The bar?" She lifts her eyebrows and small lines form across her brow. Another reminder of Ryker.

I shake my head. "Not happening."

"You don't think it's time?"

"I've been back for just over two weeks."

"And?" she prompts.

"And I've been back for just over two weeks."

She sighs. "I'm just saying that the sooner you get out there again, the sooner you'll realize he's not coming for you."

I look down at my coffee as I jiggle the handle, watching as ripples pass over the liquid. "You don't know that."

"But you don't know that he is. It would be stupid of him to do anything. He's probably moved onto someone else."

"Well, that makes it okay then, if he's moved onto some other poor girl."

She reaches across and stills my hand with her own. "That's not what I meant, and you know it. I just want to see the old you again. I want to see your smile. I want to hear your laugh."

I sit up straight and plaster on a smile.

She sighs again, admitting defeat. "Fine. I guess it is too soon. I only wanted to help. I even asked Remy and Sebastian to come down so they could come with us and act as your personal protectors."

"You're still with that guy?"

She frowns. "Why wouldn't I be?"

I grin and chew on my bottom lip. "No reason."

"No." Her eyes flash. "What do you mean by that? Don't you like him? Have you seen him?"

I hold my hands up, protesting my innocence. "Yes, yes, he's very good looking. I'm sure he's lovely."

"Lovely? He's far from lovely. Fuck lovely." She spits the word out as though it's a curse. "And good looking? You've seen him, right? He's like a fucking Greek god." She shakes her head in disbelief. "Lovely." She snorts then looks back at me questioningly. "Don't you like him?"

I laugh at how frustrated she is. "He just doesn't seem your type."

"And what exactly is my type, oh knowledgeable one?"

"Someone with a personality."

"Hey!" she cries in mock indignation. Then she settles back into her seat. "Okay, so he's a little on the dull side, but he is freakishly good in bed." She wiggles her eyebrows as though it gives added emphasis. "Speaking of boyfriends…" She lets the word hang between us.

"What?" I ask dryly.

"Remy was so worried about you."

"So you've said."

"He was," she insists. "I've never seen him like that before. He asks about you all the time."

"That's nice."

"You're not even the tiniest bit interested? I know he's my brother and all and I'm really not keen on being his pimp, but he really was worried about you. It was almost sweet."

"You are the only person in the world who would think discussing a possible boyfriend only two weeks after someone got home from being held captive was okay."

"So is that a no?"

"Yes."

She frowns playfully. "It's a yes?"

"No. It was a yes to my answer being no."

Picking up her cup of coffee, she grins over the rim. "Now you're not even making sense." She takes a noisy slurp. "Well I've already sorted for Remy and Sebastian to come down for the night, so we can either have a nice intimate time watching a movie or something with Remy sitting and staring awkwardly at you all night, or we could go to the bar." She shrugs. "Your choice."

"You're an ass, you know that?"

She smiles, the foam of the coffee caught on her upper lip. "Yes, actually, I do."

Mum is standing at the kitchen sink when I walk in the door.

"Did you have a nice afternoon with Roxy?" she asks.

I throw my bag onto the couch and flop onto one of the seats around the table. "She wants me to go out tonight."

Mum stops what she is doing and turns to look at me. "And how do you feel about that?" She dries her hands on a tea towel and sits down opposite me, watching as my head sinks into my hands.

"I don't know," is my muffled reply. "She says I should face my fear."

"And exactly which fear is she referring to?" She prises my fingers apart to catch my eye. "Does she know you won't hold a spider?"

I smile and remove my hands. "That's exactly what I told her."

Mum relaxes back into her chair, flicking the tea towel over her shoulder. "Great minds and all that."

"What do you think I should do?"

"I think you should do whatever makes you feel the best. You've only been home a matter of days. There is no point in pushing things. I'm sure Roxy means well, but she has no idea what you've been through. You are the only one who knows that."

"So you don't think I should go?"

Getting up from the table, Mum walks back over to the sink to bury her hands in the bubbles. "That's not what I said."

"You think I shouldn't?"

"Mia." She twists her head to look back at me. "Only you can answer that."

A timer beeps and Mum pulls her hands out of the water to open the oven door. She's been baking non-stop since my return. I think she needs to go back to work. The scent of oven-fresh croissants wafts through the house.

"You hungry?"

I shake my head, pulling myself up from the table. "I think I'm going to go."

Mum doesn't react. She doesn't act shocked, or surprised, she doesn't nod with approval. She merely dumps the tray of croissants on top of the oven.

"Would you like me to come along with you? Will you sing? I've never actually heard you sing anywhere other than church."

I shake my head, panic striking me even at the mention of singing. It's what drew him to me. I feel like if I did it again, it would almost be inviting his attention.

"Roxy is bringing her brother and her boyfriend along as personal bodyguards. I will be fine." But then the panic overwhelms me again and I sink back into the chair. "Maybe I shouldn't go. Part of me feels like I'm just asking for trouble."

Mum's whips around to face me. "Don't you ever say that, Mia Cooper."

"Say what?"

"That you're asking for trouble. Nothing you could ever do would be asking for someone to take you, to think they could own you!"

"I didn't mean it like that, I just meant that maybe I should just concentrate on staying safe for a while."

"I think you should stop thinking about what you should and shouldn't do and just do what you want." She sits back at the table and takes my hands between her own. "You need to take as much time as you want to heal but you also can't let fear dictate your life. You need to do things because you want to do them, Mia. Not because Roxy wants to, not because you're scared. You know I will always support your choices, but I want them to be yours, Mia."

I swallow the tears and the panic and manage a wobbly smile. "So, what you're really saying is you think I should go."

Grabbing the tea towel from over her shoulder she flicks it in my face. "Go. Stay. I don't care which, as long as it's the choice you have made and not because of anyone else."

"Right." Somehow, I feel bolder, as though some of Mum's strength has transferred to me. "I'm going to go."

Mum smiles. "Good. But make sure you have your phone on you and are with either Roxy or Remy at all times, okay?"

Getting to my feet, I walk across the space to kiss my mother on her forehead. "There's the mother I know and love."

She laughs and pushes me away, but when I look back at her, there are tears in her eyes.

"Are you okay?"

She smiles tightly and nods. "I'm fine. I'm fine." Waving her hand in front of her face, she attempts to fan away the tears. "I was such a mess while you were gone." Bursting into tears, she slides down the wall, dissolving into a mound of sobs. "I'm sorry," she wails. "I've been trying to be so strong for you. I've been through nothing compared to you and I wanted to be the strong one. Your rock, you know, the one person you could always count on for both comfort and strength. But I'm just so tired. Any time I forget, even if it's for a second, a crushing guilt overwhelms me. How could I let this happen to my baby? Why didn't I keep you safe?"

I crouch beside her and take her in my arms. "You don't have to be strong for me, Mum. You just have to be here. And you always have. Always."

Mum smiles through her tears and attempts to wipe them away, smudging her mascara in the process. "Look at me acting all stupid." She fans her face. "I need to get a grip on myself."

I shrug. "It's actually nice to see someone else losing it a little."

Mum laughs, tears all gone, and stands, holding her hands out to help me to my feet. "We're a strange lot," she says.

"What do you mean?"

"Well, we keep on trying to hold onto this blame and guilt for what happened. I've tried to stop you from doing it and yet, right here and now, I feel guilt for not keeping you safe. It's stupid. The only villains in this story are the men who took you." She pats my shoulder as she walks back over to the tray of croissants. "They are the ones who should be carrying all of the guilt. Not us." She turns to look at me. "Hungry?"

I shake my head but Mum ignores me, slicing open one of the croissants and reaching into the fridge to stuff it with ham and cheese.

"Have you heard anything more from the police?"

I shake my head again. "I would have told you if I had."

"It seems strange that they can't find anything. You've given them a description of the building and even identified one of the men. You'd think that would mean something."

"Marcel told me…" Mum looks up sharply. It must be strange for her to hear their names so easily fall from my lips. "He told me that my requestor was from a wealthy family. It wouldn't surprise me if they had people within the force keeping an eye on things. People like that tend to stick together."

A plate with the croissant sitting neatly in the middle gets placed on the table. "So have you made up your mind?"

I look over at my mother, so strong, so brave and fearless and nod my head with more resolve than I feel. "I'm going."

# CHAPTER EIGHTEEN

## MIA

When Roxy knocks on the front door, I am still in my bedroom, trying to figure out what to wear. It's never been an issue before. I wore whatever I felt like from the choice of the few dresses in my wardrobe or the selection of jeans and tops. But now, everything feels like it would be a statement.

Wearing the red dress isn't an option. Anything red I own is destined for the charity shop. I don't want that color anywhere near me. Every outfit I pull out has something wrong with it. The neckline is too revealing. The pants are too tight. The color draws too much attention.

Not only am I worried that he might be out there somewhere, watching me, I am worried who will see me. I have seen the looks from people on the odd times I have been outside the house. There are looks of pity, looks of shock, but mainly there are looks of suspicion.

If what she claims is true, why is she not hiding in her house with all the doors locked and keeping herself safe?

Why is she dressing like that and inviting attention?

Why is she smiling?

Shouldn't she still be cowering in fear under the blankets of her bed?

In the end, I blindly shove my hands into the pile of discarded clothing and pull a shirt over my head. I don't even look in the mirror as I tug on my jeans, and instead, leave the room without a backward glance.

Roxy, Remy, and Sebastian stand awkwardly in the kitchen with my mother and father. Dad stands between the two men, arms crossed and not hiding the fact that he doesn't like either of them. Remy's eyes are cast toward the ground, but when I walk in, he lifts them hesitantly and nods in my direction.

Sebastian strides forward confidently, extending his hand. "Sorry to hear about your situation," he says stiffly and attempts a smile, emphasizing his perfectly white teeth.

When Roxy first introduced us, I thought he was handsome. Devastatingly handsome. Now, I'm not so fooled by a pretty face. Marcel had a pretty face.

I allow him to shake my hand and then laugh nervously, as though my situation is something to find amusing. Roxy rolls her eyes and loops her arm through her boyfriend's as Remy steps forward to stand uncomfortably by my side. Dad narrows his eyes and Remy takes a step back.

"Have you got your phone?" Dad asks me, pulling me away from the waiting group.

"Yes, Dad." I smile to reassure him. "And it's fully charged."

"And what about that spray? Have you got it in your bag?"

I nod.

"And you'll stay with Roxy and the boys all night? You won't get separated, you won't even go to the bathroom by yourself?"

I hold my hand up with mock severity. "I solemnly swear not to use the bathroom by myself."

"And you'll call me if you need anything."

I pull him into a hug and whisper in his ear. "I'll be fine, Dad. It will be good for me to be out and about. Good for me to feel normal again."

I let go and head toward the door with more confidence than I feel.

"It's too soon," I hear my father mutter to my mother.

My mother replies with a smile stretched over her face that belies the worry lines between her eyes. "It's her decision." She nods firmly at my father before turning a beaming smile back at me. "Have a wonderful night."

"What time will you be home?" Dad asks, only to be slapped by my mother playfully. "Make sure you're safe!" he yells as the door shuts.

"Don't say that! You're implying that her safety..." her voice fades as we walk to the car.

Remy opens the back door for me, smiling hesitantly and I

climb inside and take a deep breath to calm my nerves.

"I'll look after you," he says as he sits beside me.

I shift just a fraction away from him, needing the distance between us to still my beating heart. A fine sheen of sweat covers my body and I tug on my shirt repeatedly, allowing the material to create a fan to blow cool air onto my face.

Remy's hand creeps across the seat to rest on my knee and I jerk away, startled by the touch even though I watched it happen.

"Sorry," he says. "I didn't mean anything by it." He seems slightly annoyed and shuffles closer to the door on his side, turning to look out the window.

"It's not you," I reply. "I'm just—" I don't finish. He's not looking at me anyway.

The windows of the bar are crowded with people as we pull into the carpark. I start chewing on my lip nervously, and my legs shake of their own accord. With a deep breath, I open the door and climb out with a smile stretched over my face. Roxy loops her arm through mine and tugs me toward the entrance.

"You've got this," she says as the music grows louder, but my quivering insides disagree. "We're going to have a great night."

The music is loud, and the dim light makes it hard to see. The bar is busier than I've ever seen it before, and there are many strange faces who stare back at me. I tell myself that I'm imagining the suspicious looks and the raised eyebrows.

I tell myself that every time a person leans in close to speak to the person next to them, they are not talking about me.

Remy shouts in my ear, and instinctively, I jerk away. He rolls his eyes, motioning drinking with his hand. "What do you want?" he yells over the music.

I shake my head, then change my mind and yell back to him. "Water."

He gives me the thumbs up before weaving his way through the crowd.

"Where did all these people come from?" I shout across to Roxy. She's standing beside Sebastian, her arms looped around his waist as he looks with disdain across the room. He's a city boy through and through.

"Your disappearance sort of helped the profile of this place," she shouts back.

"Really?"

I would have thought the disappearance of someone would discourage people from coming here, not increase the patronage so much that it's even difficult to find the space to breathe.

She nods. "Some reporter did a story and boom!" She motions an explosion with her hands. "Suddenly this dive is the place to be! I think I even…" her voice gets muffled by the band coming onto the small stage and strumming the strings of an electric guitar into the microphone.

"What?" I step closer in order to hear Roxy.

"I think I even caught a reporter at your house trying to

look through the windows!"

A shudder runs through me at the mere thought of being watched.

Remy comes back through the crowd, holding four glasses above his head. He hands me one and I take a sip, shuddering again when the taste of vodka and lemonade slides down my throat.

"I asked for water."

"What?" He taps his ear, indicating for me to lean closer.

"I asked for water." I swallow the knot of panic that's begun to pulse in the pit of my stomach.

"I didn't think you actually meant it." His words are hot against my ear, and I squeeze my eyes shut.

"Why would I say it if it wasn't what I meant?"

"What?" he yells back.

"Why would I—" There's nothing but confusion on his face so I drop it and cautiously sip.

I stick close to Roxy as she consumes drink after drink, eventually leading me onto the dance floor. The glass of vodka has turned warm in my hand. The boys stay in the corner we had occupied, watching us from afar. Remy glances over cautiously, while Sebastian glares at us as though we are doing something wrong.

"You good?" Roxy yells.

I smile or grimace and sort of shrug as a response. There's no point telling her that every time a stranger bumps into me, my heart starts to race. Or that every time I catch the eye of a man watching me across the crowd, a nauseated feeling creeps into my gut. Even the way Roxy's boyfriend is glaring at us makes me uneasy. I wish the guy would smile or something. He has one hell of a resting bitch face.

The band quietens as the song draws to a close, and the lead singer spits into the microphone as he talks.

"We're just going to take a quick break," he announces. Then he catches my eye and gives a wave of recognition. "But I've just spotted someone in the crowd who has graced this stage a few times before, so maybe, if we cheer loud enough she will agree to sing again. What do you say?"

The crowd erupts into thunderous applause, not because they know who I am, but because the man behind the microphone tells them to. He stands there, throwing his own cheers into the microphone as I'm gripped by fear.

I start shaking my head. My heart races and my legs tremble as the people around me start pushing me toward the stage. I reach back, straining to grab onto any part of Roxy that I can, but she just smiles and mouths that everything will be fine. Of course, she doesn't know what I know. She doesn't know he called me his songbird.

The crowd carries, pushes and shoves me to the stage and I stare out at the darkness, blinded by the spotlight that shines onto the small raised platform they call a stage.

I wonder if they can see my fear, if they can taste it or smell it like I can. I wonder if they care.

"You right, love?" the band's lead singer asks me. I know

his name. I've heard it many times before, but it escapes me as I stand frozen. "You want a backing track or something?"

I'm not sure if I respond. All I know is that he leaves and I'm alone on the stage, too scared, too petrified to move. I try to scan the crowd, looking for those eyes that glared back at me weeks before, but I'm greeted with nothing but the blaring light. Finally, when they focus a little, I make out Roxy shoving her way through the crowd, the realization of my fear finally dawning on her. She pushes and shoves, but no one notices as they gather closer to the stage, some sort of chant on their lips.

Then someone yells for them to be quiet and the room shifts. The yelled chants turn to hushed whispers. The bustle and jostle of the crowd still. All eyes turn to me.

Someone clears their throat.

Another person lets out a whoop of encouragement.

My name is yelled into the silence.

Closing my eyes, I try to block them all out. For the briefest of moments, I long to be back within the walls of the cell, for the known safety of Ryker instead of the unknown dangers of this small town.

My voice is small and trembling as I start to sing. I keep my eyes closed, thinking of Ryker as the words to 'Iris' by the Goo Goo Dolls spill from my mouth.

The world vanishes, and I'm taken back to lying in Ryker's arms, the feel of his lips as he pressed a kiss to my head. Tears rip my throat and my words with the knowledge that I will never feel like that again. I will never have his arms around me. I will never be surprised by the softness of his lips.

And then I break, the melody turning to sobs as I jump down from the stage and push myself through the crowd, yelling and screaming at those who refuse to move out of my way. The walls are closing in. The lights are too bright and somehow too loud as though their buzzing is louder than the murmurs of the crowd. I bump into someone and terror holds me in its grasp as I look up into eyes that I'm certain belong to my requestor.

"No," I gasp as hands reach for my shoulders and hold me in place.

"Who were you singing to?" the voice asks.

I keep shaking my head, my eyes closed as though there's a blindfold covering them, wrenching against the grip on my shoulders.

"Mia!" someone shouts. "Mia are you okay?" The hands disappear. "She won't talk to me," the voice continues.

"I've got her." And then Roxy's arms are around me and I lean into her, sobbing with relief. "It was just Sebastian," she says. "You're okay. You're okay." She turns to talk to someone else. "You shouldn't have grabbed her like that! We need to get outside. She needs to breathe."

As soon as she says the words, I become aware of myself and the panicked sobs of breath I keep taking. I'm aware of them, but I can't stop them. I can't control the waves of confusion or the knife of fear that's stabbed into my heart. Remy and Sebastian lead the charge as Roxy takes me outside, all the time keeping me wrapped securely in her arms.

It's not until I'm standing and staring at the stars that my breath calms and my body stops trembling.

"This was a stupid idea. I'm so sorry, Mia. I didn't know— I didn't think…" She smooths my hair, stroking her hand over my head just like my mother would do. "I'm so sorry," she says.

"Did you see him?" Remy asks, and for the first time, I see true concern on his face and begin to feel foolish for the panic that overwhelmed me.

"No. It was nothing. I just—"

"Shh," Roxy says. "It's okay. It was my fault. I pushed too hard too quickly. I don't know what I was thinking."

Taking a deep breath, I sink to the gravel, not caring when the small stones dig into my flesh. "Everyone saw." The words get caught in my throat. "Everyone will talk—"

"Let them." Roxy holds her hands out, urging me to get back to my feet. "Who cares about them? If they have anything to say they can say it to me. It was my fault. I should have never even suggested this."

A small laugh escapes and it feels so much better than the fear and panic. "I'm the one who said yes. You didn't force me, Roxy." I allow her to pull me back to my feet as I wipe the dust off my backside. "I think I should just go home.

You guys stay here. Enjoy yourselves. I'll call a taxi."

"No," Sebastian objects. "I will take you."

They almost carry me to the car. I slink inside and rest my head against the coolness of the window, my eyes lifting involuntarily to the stars scattered across the sky and wonder if my life would ever be the same again.

# requestor

# CHAPTER NINETEEN

## REQUESTOR

She's singing to me, taunting me, begging me to come and make her my own. The lyrics call out to me, telling me of her yearning, her desire to be mine. But despite her call, despite my desire to rip her from the stage and to finally claim her, I stay where I am, ignoring the buffoons that surround me and concentrating on nothing but her.

She's dressed simply for the occasion. A black top that catches the light and turns it to glitter. Jeans so tight they hug the shape of her, forcing me to imagine what it would feel like to peel them from her skin.

Her voice has changed from the last time I heard her sing. There's a pain and honesty that wasn't there before. And it's because of me. She should be on her knees, thanking me for this gift I have granted her. The gift of her voice. The gift of her freedom.

But it won't be long now.

I have made my plans.

I've been a patient man; weeks have passed since she slipped from my grasp, but soon, she will be mine. It will make all the pain and frustration, all the anger and rage worth it.

Just the thought of it alone starts my blood tingling. I take in a deep breath and let it out slowly, closing my eyes and losing myself to the sound of her voice. I imagine myself fighting my way to her, the crowd attempting to protect her from my advances. I throw punch after punch, people falling like flies around me until I reach her and pluck her from the stage. She comes to me willingly, knowing who I am, longing to be in my arms. Even the blond-haired twins that guard her can't stop me. Like fucking Prince Charming, I carry her from the bar and out to the car. No one attempts to stop me. They all fear me, cowering in the shadows like the useless fools they are. The arms of my songbird would wrap around my neck. Anyone else's touch and I would recoil, but not her. Not my songbird.

We would go home, and she would beg for me to take her, plunge into her until she screamed in ecstasy and pain. But I would deny her, choosing instead to bind her and explore her body, whispered pleas falling from her lips as my touch became perverted with pain.

I shift uncomfortably as I think about it, needing to adjust my stance to stop my arousal from becoming noticed. But I can't stop my thoughts, they have gone too far. I allow myself this indulgence, even though it risks my strength to resist taking her. I have been strong for so long. It would be a shame to ruin it all now.

So I take a deep breath and push the thoughts from my mind, sating the hum of my blood with the promise that soon she will be mine. The wait will be worth it. My patience will be rewarded.

Warm fingers thread through mine and squeeze tightly. The touch agitates me, starting the compression of anxiety in my chest. I want to squeeze back, hard, so hard I crush the fingers between mine. So hard that she begs for mercy, the pain twisting her movements and causing her to fall to her knees before me. I would step over her like the trash she is and run to my songbird.

But I must not be distracted. I have waited too long to remove my mask now.

My songbird's voice falters, cracking and wavering until sobs wrench from her body and she jumps from the stage, pushing her way through the crowd. She is so close to me. Right in front of me. The urge to take her is so strong that my body trembles under the command not to lift her into my arms.

But I will wait.

I will be patient, even though it pains me.

Because soon, my songbird will be mine.

And nothing else matters.

mia

# CHAPTER TWENTY

## MIA

I keep having the same dream. I'm in a dark room. Panic creeps over me, prickling my skin and turning my blood to ice. I'm in chains, strung up and balancing on my tiptoes. Nothing but darkness surrounds me. And then I hear it. A shushing sound. A whisper.

The light blinks on, blinding me. I shut my eyes against its intensity, seeing nothing but blotches of red mixed with flashes of white. And then I see him, lying on the floor, a pool of blood creeping out from under where the knife handle protrudes from his shoulder.

"Ryker?"

Dark eyes move to fix on me. He shakes his head, a single finger coming up to pose at his mouth. "Shh," he says.

"Ryker?" I strain at the chains around my wrists, wrenching my body, trying to escape so I can get to him.

"Shh," he says again. "Don't say a word."

His face twists, morphing into something different. Something with darker hair and paler skin. Marcel. He lifts himself from the ground, the knife gone, but blood still smeared across his naked body.

My head starts to shake. "No," I say. "Don't come near me." But there is no escape, no hiding as he stalks toward me, his smile slick with malice.

"Don't say a word." He starts to laugh. "Don't say a word." He's closer now. Close enough to reach out and touch me. "Don't say a word." His finger strokes my arm. "Don't say a word." His face is so close now, his lips only moments away from mine, curled into a sneer.

I scream.

And that's when I wake.

I've been home, I've been safe for three weeks but each night my nightmare wakes me.

Tonight is no different.

My screams are deafening but a few moments pass before I realize they're coming from my mouth. My screams turn to tears. Mum runs into my room, hair in disarray, concern framing her eyes.

"Mia." She reaches out, her hand smoothing back the hair plastered to my forehead. "Mia, it's okay. You're safe. You're safe."

It takes me a while to remember where I am. Home. Safe. In my own bed. The light from the hallway peeks through the crack of the open door. Open because I can't stand to have it closed. Open because I need the light. I need to see. To know I'm safe.

"Shh," she says, her words taking me back to my nightmare. "Shh, it's okay, it's okay."

Pulling up the covers, she climbs into bed with me, holding me close as the tears subside. I thought once I was free, my nightmares would be over. But, instead, I am trapped in a state of the unknown, a state of nervous terror because he is still out there.

And I still don't know who he is.

Three weeks can seem like a lifetime or a blink. It's been three weeks since I've been home. Almost the same amount of time that I was away. Once, my parents took me on a family vacation and we went to the Gold Coast of Australia for two weeks. The holiday went so quickly, but it seems strange to even compare it as the same amount of time I was a captive. During that time, I went through a lifetime of emotions which has turned everyday life into something confusing and frightening.

But despite my nightmares, I have been getting better, even though my attempt of returning to the bar from where I was taken was a disaster. I've ventured outside, gone to the coffee shop with Roxy, headed to the library to get more books to keep my brain occupied, and, next week, I've even said I want to start back at the bakery.

It's time to return to my old life. My life before a stranger requested me. Life before Marcel stole from me. Life before Ryker.

Even though it is only 6am, Mum and Dad have already

been at the bakery for hours when I get out of bed. Rummaging through my drawers, I pull out my bathing suit and stuff it into my bag with a towel. I used to find comfort in the silence of the water and I am determined to find it again.

The sun is rising above the roofs of my neighborhood as I stroll down the footpath. My eyes scan the area, jumping at every strange noise or flash of movement, and I have to internally remind myself that I am safe. But I keep my fingers clutched around my cell phone, ready in case I need to call for help. Just to be safe.

There aren't many people about at this time of day, but ahead of me, I see my neighbors walking their dog, their little girl, Libby, walking between them talking animatedly. Her eyes grow wide when she spots me and she breaks away from her parents, running toward me with her arms thrown wide.

"Mia!" I bend low so she can wrap her arms around me. "Where have you been? I haven't seen you in forever." She draws out the word 'forever', exaggerating it dramatically.

I hug her tightly, relishing the way her innocence feels in my arms. I used to babysit her each Friday after she finished school while her parents were still at work. We were teaching each other the piano. Well, I was watching tutorials and doing my best to pass on what I'd learned. So far, we hadn't got past lullabies, but we had a lot of fun learning. Seeing her again makes me ache for that time.

"Libby, I've missed you." I pull away and hold her at arm's length examining her dress. Libby adores pretty dresses and is was my duty to inspect them. "Pretty," I say, nodding seriously. "Very, very pretty." My eyes narrow in on the pattern displayed over the blue material, noticing there are little birds surrounded by musical notes. I swallow the knot of panic in my throat and force myself to smile wider. "How are you getting on with the piano playing? Any progress?"

She crosses her arms over her chest. "No," she says grumpily. "Because you haven't been here to teach me."

I laugh at her sass just as her parents reach us. They smile, but their smiles are tight. Libby's mother holds out her hand, waving it for Libby to take.

"Mia, it's good to see you." She draws Libby close to her side, almost shielding her from me. "I hope you are…" Her lips thin out as she smiles even tighter. "I hope you are well. I hope you are okay."

The dog bounds toward me but Libby's father tugs on the leash, forcing it back into submission.

"Where are you going?" Libby asks.

"I'm just heading to the pool for a swim."

"Can I come?"

I look up at her parents. "Of course you can, if it's okay with your parents."

Some company would do me good, keep my mind from wandering to places it shouldn't. I wouldn't get quite as much exercise with Libby trailing along behind me, but the thought of just splashing in the water and having fun appeals.

"Mia looks as though she's busy." Her mother's knuckles are white as they grasp Libby's hand. "Another time maybe."

"Oh, I really don't mind," I say, but they walk around me, determined to get back on their way. It strikes me as a little odd as Libby's mother was always keen for some extra alone time when I'd offered in the past. Libby can be a handful, but she is just the sort of handful I need at the moment. The perfect distraction.

"No, no. It's quite alright."

Libby's father gives me an apologetic smile and tugs the dog's leash.

"Would you like me to start looking after her on Fridays again? I'm feeling much better now."

"Thank you." Libby's mother keeps walking. "But we made other arrangements while you were away."

While I was away. I know she's just putting it that way to avoid unwanted questions from her daughter, but something has changed. She doesn't want me around Libby. Even though I was the one stolen and held captive, to her, I still represent some sort of danger.

Libby turns with her hand still in her mother's and waves. I wave back, hiding my sadness behind a smile.

My renewed determination to return to normal life fades with each step they take. Life will never be normal again.

Not for me. And not for those around me. What I went through will forever scar me, even if those scars aren't visible.

I walk the rest of the way to the pool briskly, my thoughts stuck on Libby's innocent smile. It is hard not to feel bitterness toward her parents, but in some small way, I can understand them. They knew what had happened to me. I guess they looked at me and imagined it could be their own daughter one day. I would want to keep her as far away as possible too.

After reaching the pool and changing into my bathing suit, I stand at the edge of the water and take a deep breath. Lifting my arms above my head and stretching onto my toes, I push myself off the side and plunge into the still water. I swim for as long as I can, holding my breath, kicking furiously with my peaked fingers slicing through the water in front of me. I keep going until my lungs burn, until they scream for air, and then I kick faster until my fingers feel the concrete and I've reached the other side. Only then do I allow myself to rise to the surface and suck in air. It feels glorious.

Glancing around the pool, I notice someone walking toward the water on the other side. Him. The man from the pool. He waves when he sees me, and my heart beat sounds loudly in my ears. Quickly, I look around to make sure we're not alone, and spot a lifeguard sitting high on a chair, staring at his phone. At least he would hear me scream.

Instead of getting into the pool, he walks around the edge toward me.

"You're back," he says, grinning from ear to ear.

"I'm back," I repeat and give him an awkward laugh, pretending my shallow breaths are from exertion alone.

Pulling his goggles up onto his forehead, he sinks down to sit on the edge of the pool. "I read about you in the papers. Are you okay?"

It's the first time anyone but my family, Roxy or the police, have addressed it directly. He doesn't shy away from the topic, doesn't walk in the opposite direction.

"Yeah," I say, not really wanting to discuss it. "I'm good." I plaster on a smile, hoping it will convince him that it isn't a lie when it is.

He jumps into the water with a plop and I unconsciously move away from him. He spits into his goggles, rubbing the saliva into the lenses before rinsing it off in the water.

Without any further discussion, he kicks off against the wall and starts to swim. A little bubble of elation blooms within me. Maybe things can return to normal after all.

# CHAPTER TWENTY-ONE

## MIA

I feel good after my swim. Refreshed and hopeful. The stretch of my muscles and the screams of my lungs kept my mind occupied. Not once did I think of my requestor out there waiting for me. Nor did I think of Ryker.

I start humming on my walk back home, humming which soon turns into quiet singing. The sun, now higher in the sky, warms my skin, soaking into me as though it is happiness itself. As I walk past the entrance to the small park, birds chirp noisily, and the sound of children laughing as they play reaches my ears. I pass a bush and a dog leaps out, tongue wagging, almost smiling as it bounds away from its frustrated owner.

I don't jump. I don't even flinch.

The sun stays in the sky, the world doesn't darken. I am okay. Perhaps not completely okay, but I'm getting there.

But as soon as I turn onto the street that leads to mine, my singing is joined by a beat. Footsteps echo off the concrete behind me.

And I'm back at square one, my heart pounding faster as I imagine the stranger behind me as him. My requestor. Part of me keeps waiting for him to appear, almost as though I expect it. But I tell myself that I'm fine. Because I am. No hands have reached to grab me. It's probably just a person out for a morning stroll with no idea of what their footsteps are doing to me.

Even still, I reach into my pocket and wrap my hands around my phone, reminding myself that safety and reassurance is only a phone call away. I've programmed my phone to dial my mother, my father, Roxy and the police at the touch of a number.

But despite my reassurance, my heart keeps racing in my chest and I quicken my steps. My panic spikes when the steps behind me quicken too. I hazard a glance behind, mainly to assure myself that my imagination is running away, and that's when I see him.

The man from the bar.

The one with the hungry eyes.

He smiles at me sadistically and begins to run.

Lurching myself forward, I sling my bag over my back and start to sprint. Fumbling inside my pocket, I bring out my phone, my fingers shaking as I attempt to push the button. It rings and rings as I silently pray for my mother to answer, the sound accenting the panic inside me, but before anyone can answer, I trip and my phone falls to the ground, skidding out of my reach and the screen shattering.

Terror takes hold and I toss my bag aside as I stumble back to my feet, removing all burdens to allow me to run faster. My house is still far away, but Roxy's is closer, so I turn down her street, not caring as tears begin streaming down my face and blurring my vision.

My requestor toys with me, increasing and decreasing his pace to match mine, gaining on me slowly. My heart pounds. My legs quiver and shake as I force myself forward, pleading for safety. I glance behind me again, because part of me feels like this isn't real, like I'm stuck in one of my nightmares, but he is still there with the sadistic smile spread over his face even as he runs.

My glance backward costs me, and I stumble, my hands hitting the ground with force, but I manage to get up again, running toward Roxy's house. I can see it in the distance. Safety. All I need to do is get there with enough time to grab the spare key, insert it into the lock, and slam the door shut behind me. Once inside, I can hide and call the police. The thought pushes my legs faster and my strides longer. But his steps keep thundering behind me.

A car pulls out of Roxy's driveway and my heart soars, thinking it is her, but the car isn't the same sleek blue one that was parked outside my house. But when the driver of the car sees me, he swerves to the side of the road, opening the door and jumping out before it even comes to a complete stop. The car keeps rolling forward and bumps into the gutter as Roxy's boyfriend races past me, straight toward the man chasing me. There's a look of contempt on the man's face as he turns abruptly, racing the other way when he realizes we are no longer alone. I watch as they turn the corner, Sebastian chasing after my requestor as though his life depends on it.

And I just stay there, frozen on the footpath as waves of terror and relief roll through me as nausea.

He's here.

He's been watching this whole time, waiting until I was alone.

My eyes stay stuck on where they disappeared until Sebastian rounds the corner again, chest heaving with exertion. He meets my eye and shakes his head. I crumple to the ground, feeling as though all the blood has been drained from me. Sebastian races over, bending down to take me in his arms, but when he notices the way I'm cowering and trembling, he just kneels beside me.

"It's okay, Mia," he says, keeping a safe distance between us. "He's gone now. You're safe."

But I'm not safe. I will never be safe with him out there watching and waiting. Sebastian shuffles forward, tentatively reaching out to lay his hand on my shoulder.

"Come on. We can't stay here."

It's only then that I realize I'm cowering in the middle of the road. Taking Sebastian's hand, I allow him to pull me to my feet, though I'm still shaking and trembling, and my breath is coming out in short quick pants. It feels as though

I'm suffocating and no matter how hard I try, I can't breathe.

Sebastian leads me over to the car, opening the back door and lowering me to the seats. I flinch when he reaches across me, and he apologizes, showing me a bottle of water and offering it to me.

"Drink this. It will help you calm down."

"I can't breathe," I manage to stutter.

"I know. It's okay. I think you're having a panic attack. Just sit there, concentrate on breathing deeply, drink the water and I'll call Roxy."

"And the police." My voice is small and weak.

He leans against the car and pulls his phone out of his pocket. Attempting to control my trembling, I twist the cap off the bottle and drink greedily, hoping it will do as Sebastian said and help calm me. The water is cool, and I try to concentrate on the feeling of it sliding down my throat. I imagine it spreading into my body, imagine myself calming, my heart beat slowing. I close my eyes but then wrench them back open when his smile stretches across my memories.

It was pure evil.

My heart starts to race again and I take another chug on the bottle drinking and drinking until nothing remains. Sebastian's voice is low and controlled as he talks to Roxy. And suddenly I'm weary. So very, very tired. Exhausted. But each time I close my eyes, he's there again, smiling at me, calling me his sweet songbird.

Sebastian walks around to the other side of the car and

pulls open the door, climbing in and sitting next to me.

"They're on their way," he says. His hand hovers in the air as though he wants to touch me, comfort me, but when he sees the renewed terror in my eye, he places it on his knee, moving closer to me so I can feel the reassurance of his presence without his touch.

"It was him?" he asks. "The one who requested you?"

Somehow hearing it out loud makes it more terrifying, more real, and I burst into tears again. This time he doesn't hesitate as he pulls me close, tucking my head beneath his chin and stroking my hair just like my mother, just like Roxy. Maybe he's not so bad after all.

The repetitive motion of his hand over my head causes my eyelids to droop. Now that I'm safe, I just want to disappear, fade away and not have to think anymore. Go to that safe place of oblivion.

It's so tempting to fall asleep, but then I think of Roxy on her way, of the police who will want to question me again, and I try to force my eyes back open.

But I can't.

Something is weighing them down. Something is weighing my whole body down, making my limbs heavy and feeling as though they are sinking into the fabric of the car.

Sebastian strokes my hair over and over. "Shh," he says. "Shh, it's going to be okay."

The world is pulling me down, closing in. Panic sparks in my chest once again. Sebastian's hand no longer feels comforting. It is hot and heavy, laced with malice as he runs it over my hair. I attempt to pull away, but my effort only causes a faint moan to come out of my mouth.

"Shh," he says again. "Don't say a word."

# sebastian

# CHAPTER TWENTY-TWO

## SEBASTIAN

The movement of the car rocks her body. Her head is in my lap and she's stretched over the back seat, her body soft and pliable. There's a slight smile on her lips as I push her hair back from her face. Even in this unconscious state, she knows she is mine.

My songbird is finally mine.

The elation that fills me is an exquisite thrill that I've never known before. My blood hisses and hums, but it's not filled with electrifying rage like it normally is. It is quiet and content, soothed with the anticipation of what is to come.

My plan had been executed well. It was almost too easy. Cameron followed her along the road and chased her right into my arms. It wasn't until the very last moments of consciousness that it dawned on her what was really happening, that she was finally where she belonged. Those big dark eyes looked into mine, droopy with the need to close, and there was a flicker of realization, a split second that the truth dawned on her before she succumbed. It was in that moment that my heart soared. I pulled her close, stroked her hair and murmured the words I know she longed to hear.

*Don't say a word.*

Her body had relaxed then and she pressed against me, needy and desperate. And it was as she fell into that blissful state that the smile passed over her lips. The smile that is still there now as she lies in my lap.

Looking upward, I catch the eye of Cameron in the rear vision mirror. He nods as though acknowledging a job well done and returns his gaze to the road. Bending down low, I press my lips to hers for the very first time. They are soft and pleasing. They taste of sin. My cock stirs, the weight of her head on my lap feeding my desire.

Gravel crunches under the tires of the car as we pull into the driveway. I snap at Cameron to be careful as he lifts her from my lap and hoists her over his shoulder. I lead the way as he carries her up the stairs and we weave through the corridors that lead to the room I have prepared for her. Her body flops onto the bed gracefully, even in sleep.

"Leave," I order Cameron, eyes fixed on my prize.

I have waited so long for this moment. I have watched from afar. I have watched from up close. I have kept my desires locked up tight as I waited for her, but now the wait is over.

She is mine.

Closing the door behind Cameron, I walk over and rip open the closet. Shuffling through the selection, I pull out a blood red dress, the material smooth and silky between my fingers, and inhale its scent. Somehow everything already smells of her. It's as though this room, and everything within it, already knows it is hers. Already knows it exists to please me.

Her limp body is hard to undress and once she's stripped naked and I have to force myself not to act upon the desire to run my hands over her skin. She's so perfect. So flawless. Any bruises and wounds she had are nothing but a faint shadow on her flesh. I slide the material over her body, both covering and emphasizing her beauty, and slip out the door. She will stay asleep for a while. The contents of the water bottle ensured it.

It's hard to wait, now that she is mine, but I will be patient, something I'm beginning to value for its addition to tension and desire. Waiting for her has been torture, but an exquisite form of it. Watching her, being so close and holding back on my urges has brought an intensity to my emotions I didn't think possible.

She never suspected that the man who requested her was the man that stood by her best friend's side. Roxy means nothing to me. She was a way to pass the time, a way to sate my urges while I waited for my songbird. She used me for my body, just like I used her. Roxy moaned for me, panted my name, screamed. She ached for me to the point that it became pathetic. Little did she know that I ached too, but it was for Mia. I wore my mask well.

The first time I met Mia, she was nothing more than the quiet girl next to Roxy. She was beautiful. She's always been beautiful. But it was hidden, muted and dulled. My blood didn't buzz at the sight of her. It was her voice that set my blood on fire. When the spotlight formed that halo around her, I knew I needed her to appease the monster within. Roxy had no idea. She was easy to deceive. A smile here, a wink there, a merciless fuck that always left her wanting more. She thought she fulfilled me. She thought she was enough. Foolish girl.

The hum of my blood is loud in my head. It feels like molten lava, simmering and boiling, ready to explode from its confines. But I must be patient. I will be patient. I want her to open her eyes and know that I am her god.

It won't be long now. Soon she will wake and realize that she has always been mine.

Keep reading for a sneak peek of

**My Sweet Songbird**

the final part in the Requested Trilogy.

# ACKNOWLEDGMENTS

Thank you for venturing along this journey to the dark side with me. I can't wait for you to read what is in store for the final book.

I want to thank the awesome team of people who help shape my stories into what they are. So to my alpha reader, my editor, and my beta readers, thank you so much!

And to you, the reader. Every copy bought, every posted comment, every review left and every email sent mean the world to me.

Thank you for your support.

SABRE

# KEEP UP TO DATE

If you'd like to keep up to date with news regarding my books, please sign up for my newsletter:

**www.subscribepage.com/sabreroseauthor**

You can also find me on social media:

**www.facebook.com/sabreroseauthor**

**www.twitter.com/sabreroseauthor**

Website:

**www.sabreroseauthor.com**

Email:

**sabreroseauthor@gmail.com**

# THE STORY CONTINUES . . .

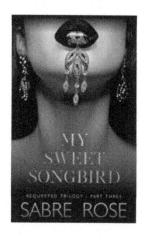

**Deceived. Stolen. Trapped.**

I thought I was free but he tricked me.

Fooled me into running straight into his arms.

Now I am his.

His to command.

His to use.

# MY SWEET SONGBIRD

## MIA

Panic. It's back. The swell of nausea, the sense of dread. Only this time when I wake, my eyes open to light, my body is cushioned in comfort and there are no chains around my wrists.

I blink. Once. Twice. And stare up at an ornate ceiling of delicate molding dancing around a chandelier. The thoughts in my head are thick and foggy, a feeling I'm familiar with, but I'm unsure why.

Sitting up, I'm surprised to find myself dressed in a red silk gown which spreads over the bed like a bloom of blood. I feel dazed. Woozy. My head thuds impossibly loud and I hold myself as still as possible and let my eyes wander. Black wallpaper covered in gold filigree patterns. A gold chandelier hanging from the ceiling. Black curtains floating in the breeze from an open window.

There's a sound at the door, a key turning in the lock, then it creaks open and he steps in. The moment I see him, memories come flooding back.

Being chased down the road.

The hard thud of feet on the pavement behind me.

The pulsing fear.

And then Sebastian. Holding me, comforting me, feeling so tired in his arms that I just wanted to sleep. But there are still parts missing. They're there in my mind, but it's like they keep slipping out of reach.

"Sebastian?" I say groggily, my voice coming out deep and foreign.

"You're awake, I see."

The panic is still there, prickling at the back of my mind. It dances on my chest, gently tapping a steady rhythm on my heart.

"What's going on?" I look around the room again, my eyes taking in the open crack of the wardrobe door, revealing a glimpse of red. "Why am I here? Where's Roxy?"

Sebastian walks over to the bed and sits on the edge, causing the mattress to dip. There's something different about him. A quiet confidence I haven't seen before. A smirk instead of a bored insolent expression. His hand snakes out to rest on my ankle, the only part of me exposed under the folds of material. It feels wrong. Strange. Hot and heavy.

My body starts to tremble.

"What's happening?" I ask again, my voice sounding a little more like my own, but cracking with fear.

He strokes my ankle gently, running his hand up and

down my leg. Jostling across the mattress, he moves closer, an excited gleam in his eye. Leaning forward, he inhales deeply.

"You're finally mine, my sweet songbird."

My heart sinks and panic drowns me. I start to shake my head, refusing to believe the truth.

"No." I keep shaking. "No. It can't be. You can't be."

He shuffles even closer, taking my hand in his and bringing it to his lips.

"Yes. We can finally be together. No more Ryker. No more Roxy. No more of my father making the rules. Just you and me like it has always meant to be."

My brain refuses to compute the information. I jerk my hand away, scrambling back to press against the headboard and draw my knees to my chest, hiding in the ruffles of red. "But Roxy," I say. "You love her."

He laughs, something I've never heard before. At another place, at another time, I might think him handsome. He's got jet-black hair, thick eyebrows and a wide mouth. His eyes are blue. But they are not blue like Ryker's are blue. They are intense and hard. Piercing.

"She's nothing. Well, no, not nothing." He strokes my cheek with the back of his finger, leaving my skin seared. "She introduced me to you, my sweet songbird, and for that, I will forever be grateful." His hand drops back to his lap. "But I never loved her. She was nothing more than a way to pass the time until you became mine."

"What do you want?" I stutter, pulling my knees tighter to my chest and trying to stop the shaking.

"You," he says. "I want you." He moves so he is sitting before me on his knees, his dark hair perfectly groomed, his teeth perfectly straight and white, his eyes gleaming. "I want your body. I want your love. I want your voice and your passion and your talent." He moves even closer, pressing his hands to my knees and shoving his face so close to mine, his breath hits my face. "I want your soul," he hisses. "I have waited so long for you. It felt like torture. I had to wait as Ryk—"

"Is he here?"

He reels back as though I have slapped him, the intensity in his eyes replaced with venom. "Forget about him. He is not important. He was merely someone to condition you because my father thought I wouldn't be able to control myself. He thought—Never mind what he thought. It doesn't matter now. You are here, and you are mine."

His eyes drop to my mouth and I unconsciously bite my bottom lip. He groans at the motion and closes his eyes just for a moment. Taking advantage of his distraction, I leap from the bed and race toward the door. Grabbing the handle, I pull, but the door is locked. I keep trying, rattling the door, but it is pointless. Tears spring to my eyes but I push them back. This is no time to cry. I need to get away. I cannot go through this again.

Sebastian lifts himself from the bed, stalking slowly

toward me. "There is no point in trying to run. This is your cage, my sweet songbird." He holds his hands out and twirls around as though I should admire the décor. "I designed it especially for you. Do you like it?"

Pressing myself against the door, my fingers still gripped around the handle as though there is hope that it might suddenly work, I hold my other hand out.

"Stay away from me."

Sebastian laughs. "Or what?" His wicked smile flashes wider. "What are you going to do? Stab me like you stabbed Ryker?"

I swallow. "Is—Is he okay?"

"Enough about Ryker!" He races toward me, wrapping his hand around my neck, and pushes me against the door until my feet rise off the floor and I'm balancing on my tiptoes.

"Do not mention him again! You are mine. Everything about your life before me no longer exists. You exist for me only, do you understand?"

His fingers cut into my throat, restricting my air. I claw at them, desperate for relief, but his grip is impossibly strong. I want to kick him, knee him, spit at him, claw his eyes out, but he is too close pressed against me. His fingers are wrapped so tightly all I can think about is my need for air.

"You are no longer Mia Cooper." He spits my name as though it is poison. "You are mine."

He lets me go and I slump to the floor, coughing and spluttering as I try to suck in air. Frantically I scan the room, looking for escape. The curtains flutter in the breeze and a faint hope rises that I might be able to jump out the window.

The anger that rippled through Sebastian a moment ago is gone, and in its place, there's someone calmer, more in control. He walks over to a plush red chair in the corner and sinks into it, draping himself over it as though it is a throne. Noting the direction of my gaze, one side of his mouth curls upward. Jerking the rope that dangles beside him, he rips the curtains open.

"Take a look," he says.

I stay on the ground, eyes darting between him and the open window. From where I'm lying on the floor, the only thing I can see out the window is blue sky, reminding me of my cell, though the window is bigger and the walls surrounding it are covered in a patterned black wallpaper, rather than cold concrete.

"Go on," he urges. "Have a look at your world."

Cautiously getting to my feet, I walk over to the window, inhaling the whiff of fresh air and look out. We are three stories high. Below me, there is nothing but fields of grass.

Sebastian gets off the chair and stands behind me, his lips brushing over my hair as he speaks. "Welcome to the Atterton Manor, my songbird. Welcome to your new home." He pushes my hair behind my ear and lowers his voice. "Do you like it?"

I turn and look into his cold blue eyes. "You're not going to get away with this."

"I'm not?" He takes a step forward and I take a step back. "I believe you'll find I already have." Sebastian smiles. It's strange to see it on him. When around Roxy, he was so quiet, so unobtrusive, but here in this room, he's transformed into someone different. He's lifted his mask and I wonder how I didn't see that he wore one before.

He raises his hand to stroke my cheek, but I jerk back, my feet getting caught in the folds of material.

Sebastian shakes his head. "Tut, tut, tut. I thought Ryker had trained you better than this."

I try to move away further, but my backside presses against the windowsill, the cool breeze drifting over the exposed skin of my back. Sebastian keeps stepping forward, pushing himself against me until I'm almost leaning out the window. "Careful," he whispers in my ear. "You wouldn't want to fall."

Without warning, he shoves my chest and I reel back, having to grab onto the sides of the window to keep from falling.

Taking a step back, he folds his arms across his chest. "See? You do want to stay."

With my fingers pressed to the wall, I slide sideways, away from him, away from the window. My heart pounds in my chest and my mouth is dry. The nauseating feeling of panic bubbles beneath the surface of my skin.

"You have to let me go, Sebastian. The police will be looking for you. They will find you."

Sebastian yanks the curtains shut and returns to his throne-like chair. "I doubt that." He holds his hand out as though inspecting his fingernails. "They didn't before. And besides, my father knows all the right people in all the right places. He's been doing this for years."

"Stealing women?"

Sebastian blinks, no hint of remorse or shame in his posture. "Yes, though I would argue the fact that you can't steal something that belongs to you, and you belong to me, Mia. But we've never taken someone from this close to home. There's something daring about it, don't you think? Thrilling."

"My parents won't give up. They will keep looking for me." I keep sliding sideways with my back to the wall, slowly making my way back to the door.

"I know."

"And what about Roxy?"

He frowns. A single line presses between his brows and a strand of his perfectly groomed hair falls out of place. "What about her?"

"What are you going to tell her about me?"

"Why would I tell her anything? I told you, she's inconsequential."

"Inconsequential?"

"There's no need to repeat what I say, Mia."

For some reason using my name sounds crueler than when he called me his songbird. It reminds me of who I am, rather than who he wants me to be.

"And you may as well get thoughts of escape out of your mind right now." He nods toward the door. "There is only one key and I have it." He tugs on the chain around his neck and a key peeks out from above his shirt. "See?" I follow the key greedily with my eyes. "You're more than welcome to come and see if you can get it."

He dangles it, swaying it back and forth. "Come on, my sweet songbird. It's right here. All you've got to do is take it."

Without giving him any more time to prepare, I launch myself toward him, a tornado of fists and fury. He rises to meet me and laughs when I hit him. I punch and I kick and I flail until he engulfs me with his arms, holding me against him tightly, reminding me that I am no match for him. His heartbeat pounds and vibrates through me.

"Did you like that?" he asks, breathing heavily against my ear. His tongue slides over my neck and groans. "Because I sure did." He chuckles as I struggle and licks me again. "You taste so good, my sweet songbird. So good. So innocent. So sweet. Did you know I was the one who told Ryker not to hurt you? Did he tell you that? Did you know that I was the one who gave him the rules for your training?"

I keep struggling, straining to release myself from his arms, but the more I struggle the tighter he holds. "You might think that was because I didn't want to hurt you," his voice lowers to a sinister whisper, "but you'd be wrong."

I try to jostle free my elbow and ram it into his side, but he maneuvers his body away while still holding me tight. "Keep struggling. I like it." He laughs coldly. "But the only reason I told him those things was to stop him hurting you. The rules don't apply to me. I can do whatever I like because you're mine. Your pain is mine. Your body is mine. You. Are. Mine."

He lets go, pushing me away, and I stumble to the ground, reaching out my hands to break my fall.

"Now," he stalks toward me, "Let's see if Ryker's training was as useless as he was." He's standing directly over me now, his ice-blue eyes boring into mine. "Don't say a word."

# BOOKS BY SABRE ROSE

**Thornton Brothers**

*(Contemporary Romance Series)*

Touched

Tempted

Taken

Torn

Tears

**You Ruined Me**

*(A Tragic Dark Romance Novella)*

**Requested Trilogy**

*(Dark Romance Series)*

Don't Say A Word

Until You're Mine

My Sweet Songbird